D0064980

BREAKING BOXES

BREAKING BOXES

A. M. JENKINS

DELACORTE PRESS

Published by
Delacorte Press
Bantam Doubleday Dell Publishing Group, Inc.
1540 Broadway
New York, New York 10036

Library of Congress Cataloging-in-Publication Data
  Jenkins, A. M.
    Breaking boxes / A. M. Jenkins.
       p.   cm.
    Summary: When in the course of an unusual friendship Charlie reveals
something confidential about his brother, he must decide if he can accept
the risks of caring.
    ISBN 0-385-32513-4
    [1. Friendship—Fiction.   2. Brothers—Fiction.]   I. Title.
  PZ7.J4125Br   1997
  [Fic]—dc21   96-53626
                                                                   CIP
                                                                    AC

The text of this book is set in 12-point Adobe Garamond.

Book design by Julie E. Baker
Manufactured in the United States of America

October 1997

10   9   8   7   6   5   4   3   2   1

BVG

TO MARTHA MOORE, JAN PECK, ANDREA SCHULZ,
LIDIA ZENIDA, AND ALL MY OTHER WRITER FRIENDS
WHO TOOK TIME FROM THEIR OWN WORK TO HELP ME
BY READING, THINKING, DISCUSSING, AND QUESTIONING.

MANY THANKS TO MY EDITOR, WENDY LOGGIA—
AN EVENHANDED COMBINATION OF BUSINESS SENSE,
INTEGRITY, AND HEART.

CHAPTER 1

My brother, Trent, always makes me want to laugh. Even when I'm sitting at the breakfast table, even when my face is so asleep that only years of habit can get my mouth to open for the cold cereal my hand is shoveling in.

"You're torturing me, Charlie. You know that?" he says, measuring out his coffee. He's got his back to me. I keep scooping cereal in. "Can't you turn your alarm down just once? Or at least set it to something else. That country stuff's killing me."

Trent's always wide awake the moment his feet touch the floor. He doesn't even start making coffee until he's showered and dressed. Me, I hit the snooze button a couple of times every morning. And I take my shower the night before, so I can sleep till the last possible moment.

Trent starts singing at the counter. With his back to me. "My dawg is dead," he moans. "That ankle-gnawing mongrel. The sheriff shot him with a sawed-off, and now I don't got no dawg."

"Shut up," I say, but I can feel a grin trying to crack its way across my face.

1

Trent runs water into the coffeepot. "My wife done left me, *nair nair.*" The *nair nair* is his way of twanging like a guitar. "I hit the snooze alarm three times, and she had to hear this stupid song at seven A.M., *nair nair.*"

"Twice," I say. "I only hit it twice."

"Three times," Trent tells me, punching the start button on the coffeemaker. "Three times I had to hear Johnny Joe Billy Bob Bucket singing through his nose instead of his mouth. Now I've got some song stuck in my head. What is it? Something about boots under a bed?"

"Don't ask me," I say. "I was asleep."

"It's a plot." Trent brings his plate over to the table and sits down. He eats bagels for breakfast, I eat cereal. It's been that way ever since it's been just the two of us. "Country's trying to take over rock. Every year, a little less steel guitar, a little more percussion. Next thing you know they'll be wrecking their instruments on the stage."

"They're already doing that," I point out.

"See?"

I'm kind of starting to wake up. The steamy smell of coffee makes its way over to me. I like the smell of coffee. I just hate the taste.

I'm sitting there sniffing when it hits me. There's something I've got to warn Trent about.

"Hey," I tell him. "You might get a call at work today. I might be getting into a fight."

I can hear the coffee trickling into the pot. Trent's

bagel is in his hand; he hasn't even taken a bite of it yet but he sets it back on the plate.

"Why?"

My cereal's gone, but now's not the time to take the bowl to the sink. "Some guys've been hassling me, and I decided today I'm going to take care of it."

"What have they been hassling you about?"

I know what he's thinking. He's thinking it's got something to do with him. I look him right in the eye and tell the truth. "Nothing special. Just some rich jocks who get their jollies by acting superior."

"Are you sure that's all it is?"

"One hundred percent," I tell him.

Trent nods and takes a bite of bagel. He's a powerful guy, Trent is, lifts weights and all that, and if he wanted to, he could take those guys out with his little finger. If I asked him to, he might. But I'm not exactly scrawny myself, and even if I was, I wouldn't ask.

And Trent would never give me some stupid advice, like go tell a teacher or just ignore those guys. He knows telling a teacher would just make things worse, and he knows if I've decided to fight, that means I've already ignored it as long as I can.

Trent's one reason I look at other high-school people and I think, What a drag, having parents who give you stupid advice when they don't even have a clue what your life is like. Parents you have to lie to, because they screw things around so you have to choose between lying and getting into trouble. Trent understands that you can get into a ton worse trouble by running to teachers than by standing up for yourself.

"The school's got my work number, don't they?"

"Yeah," I say, though I'm not really sure because they've never had to call about me before. "If they don't, I'll give it to them."

"You sure you can handle this?"

"Yeah." I take my empty bowl to the sink, rinse it, and put it in the dishwasher. Trent's eating his bagel, kind of absentminded. His coffee's done; I pour him a cup and put in the creamer till it's the right color. "I'll be all right," I say as I put the cup down in front of him. "Don't worry."

"Thanks. But I will."

"I know," I tell him, picking up my books. I also know he worries about me not having a lot of friends like he does. Any friends, if you want to get technical.

And now I'm getting in a fight. I should tell him it's okay—I'm fine, I don't need anything from anybody, I don't ask anything except to be left unhassled.

Today I'm just going to have to ask a little louder, that's all.

I don't say anything, I just turn at the front door and wait till I'm sure he's looking at me. Then I nod, once. He hesitates, then nods back and even lets himself give me a little smile as I head off to school.

That's the thing about Trent and me. It doesn't take a whole lot of words to get things said.

*   *   *

It doesn't take long. Between first and second period, I have to go to my locker and there they are, the three of them. Or Luke Cottington, mostly. Old David and Brandon are just along for the ride, you can tell. Maybe I'll leave them alone, when I start.

"Hey, Charles, nice shoes."

I'd have nice shoes too, if I was a rich parasite like Cottington. He's always the first one out of the gate when it comes to being an asshole. He's in my homeroom, they all are—that's why our lockers are close together, and why all our last names start with C. Luke Cottington. David Carlson. Brandon Chase. And me, Charlie Calmont.

They haven't come over yet. Maybe they won't. Maybe they'll just stay over there, and I won't have to take care of it today.

"It's Char-*lie*," says Brandon, drawing out the last syllable. I toss my algebra folder onto the floor of my locker with the other ones. Probably I shouldn't pick anything up yet. Keep my hands free. I stand there, acting like I'm looking for something. Waiting to see what happens.

"Charlie," says Luke, right in my ear. "I like those shoes, man. You get those at Valu-Mart?"

David starts laughing. "No, man. He got them out of the Dumpster *back* of Valu-Mart."

Very funny. I won't be leaving David alone after all. I'm getting mad now. It's going to be easy.

"Hey, Charlie," says Brandon, and I feel a hand on my shoulder.

Then the hand's gone; I've knocked it away, and Brandon's staggering sideways with one hand to his mouth.

When we lived in East Texas with my mom, I spent a lot of time hanging out by myself at the community center. There was this black belt who used to teach classes in tae kwon do, and even though we never had the money for classes he showed me some stuff. And I let him, even though I usually don't like to take things from people.

So I'm not afraid. And Luke and David can't decide what to do now. Should they check on their pal Brandon or jump me?

At the same time, I can't decide what to do. Should I go after Brandon again, or try for that asshole Luke while Brandon's down? Or should I just get my stuff and go to class?

"Don't fuck with me," I tell Brandon as he straightens up. He's mad now, too, he's coming at me, but stupidlike, with his whole body instead of his fists. I can't remember how to throw him, so I just take a jab at his face, and even as he's blocking it my other fist's already buried in his stomach.

Then somebody's got me from behind and Mr. Payton, the vice-principal, has Brandon from behind, and Luke and David are acting like they're just part of the crowd, like this is a play they just happen to be watching. Some friends.

And then Brandon and I are being dragged to the office, and the funny thing is, nobody says a word.

CHAPTER 2

Mr. Payton dumps me and Brandon in his office and leaves, which I think is pretty stupid. How does he know we're not going to try to kill each other while he's gone?

So we're just sitting there, not saying anything. Brandon's all straight up in his chair, while I'm stretched out trying to make myself comfortable. Which is hard to do when there's this humongous paddle hanging on the wall behind Mr. Payton's desk. Although I think it's just for show. I think they get sued nowadays if they hit kids.

Finally Mr. Payton comes in. He goes and sits behind his desk, and he's got this stack of phone messages and infractions in his hand. You got to feel for him; it's only the third week of school and he's already behind in his work.

Mr. Payton looks at me, like he's waiting for something. I just look back at him. So he looks at Brandon.

Brandon seems kind of uptight; he won't meet Mr. Payton's eyes. I don't remember Brandon ever getting into trouble either. That's probably about the only thing we have in common. I mean, there's the rich-guy factor. And like I said, I don't have any friends at the moment, while he's on the LC, the Leadership Committee. The way they get the LC is they plug in this popularity meter, and whoever sends the needle off the scale gets to run the school. Or gets to *think* they run the school; as far as I can tell, all they do is vote about where to put trash cans and stuff like that.

But I'm thinking Brandon's popularity might work to my advantage, because if Mr. Payton doesn't do anything to Brandon because he's such a big shot and all, he can't really do anything to me, no matter how much he wants to.

"What's going on, Brandon?" Mr. Payton asks.

"We had a misunderstanding," Brandon says.

I can't help it, I have to laugh. Of course he won't tell what happened, because he started it. Or his friends did, and now that his friends have disappeared, old Chase seems about as hostile as a puppy that just wet the rug.

"Do you have something to add"—Mr. Payton shuffles through the stack in his hand and pulls out a card—". . . Charlie?"

Brandon's hands are gripping the edge of his chair. He looks like a kid waiting for a shot at the doctor's office.

"No," I say, and Brandon loses like one-twentieth of his tension. Enough to glance at me.

"I don't allow fighting in my school," Mr. Payton says, though he's only the vice-principal.

"It won't happen again, Mr. Payton," says Brandon.

Mr. Payton takes another card out of the stack. Must be Brandon's.

He checks one card, then the other. Then he lays them side by side on the desk by the phone.

"Are you going to call our parents?" Brandon asks.

"Yes, I am. To let them know what's going on."

So they do have Trent's work number. They should; he's worked at the bookstore for the past six years. Ever since he started college. I know he's embarrassed sometimes when people find out he's still in college after six years, but he shouldn't be. He makes good grades. Fantastic grades. It just takes a long time to finish college when you've got to work full-time and support a younger brother. And it's not like he's a total peon; he's an assistant manager who'd be a manager by now if they didn't know he doesn't want to work in a bookstore for the rest of his life. That's Trent for you—he'd tell the truth if it kept him from being a millionaire.

I notice Brandon's all frozen in his seat. Definitely never gotten in trouble before.

"Since this is a first offense, I'm not going to suspend you," Mr. Payton goes on.

Brandon glances at me again. I shrug at him, I don't know why.

"I'm sending you both down to OCS for three days," Mr. Payton says, making some kind of note on each card.

OCS means On-Campus Suspension. That means you sit in the same room all day, and your teachers send your assignments down, and you're not allowed to talk to anyone. I'm just relieved they're not going to call Trent away from work for this.

"Three days?" Brandon bursts out, like he can't believe it.

"Actually, it might be fair to say four, because I'm sending you down for the rest of today, as well." Payton looks at him over the rim of his glasses. "But we can make it longer, if you like."

Brandon doesn't say anything.

"I don't like fighting in my school, boys. If this happens again you will be suspended. Do you understand?"

We both nod.

"I want to hear 'Yes sir.'"

"Yes sir," we both say.

"If it happens again, I'll get mad. You don't want to make me mad."

He's tapping the cards on the desk like he's impatient to get rid of us so he can get started on his stack. His voice is really quiet and friendly, but something about it makes me agree. I don't want to make him mad. And I think adding to his workload just might do it.

"The school year's just begun. Let's make a fresh start and forget this little misunderstanding. Shall we?"

"Yes sir," Brandon says. Mr. Payton looks at me.

"Yes sir," I say.

And then we're out of there, like *yes*terday, as Trent says. Mr. Payton escorts us down to the OCS room. He's efficient, you can say that for him.

When we walk in, the only person there is the teacher. This period, it's Miss Rippen, one of the Spanish teachers. They can't afford to have a full-time guard or whatever you call it, so they round up six teachers every year and make each one volunteer to oversee a period of OCS.

I guess since it's only three weeks into the year, we're the only ones who've gotten in trouble yet. We walk in and sit down, Brandon by the door, me by the window.

"I'll have their classwork sent to you," Mr. Payton says.

"Yes, of course." Miss Rippen is a first-year teacher. That's why she was stupid enough to get stuck with OCS.

I slump down in my seat and stick my legs way out, crossing my feet. It's very quiet. I hate quiet.

"Brandon, what on earth have you been doing to get sent to the office?"

Mr. Payton is gone, and Miss Rippen looks all concerned. It figures, she already knows who Brandon is, and that he's too good to be in here. Probably he's in her Spanish class or something.

Brandon shifts in his seat, like he knows he's supposed to answer but he doesn't want to.

Miss Rippen gives him a couple of seconds, but he

keeps his eyes on his desk. Then she turns to me, but the funny thing is, she's still got that concerned look. "What about you?"

Maybe she doesn't know no one's supposed to talk in here.

"Fighting," I say. I notice how her face is kind of pretty, and she's not old at all. Maybe Trent's age, and she doesn't dress like a teacher but like a college student, kind of sloppy in a feminine way. I mean, she's wearing a skirt and all, but her blouse is loose-fitting and it's not buttoned all the way up. In fact, I can almost see some cleavage. Just almost.

I realize she's still looking at me, so *I* get busy looking out the window.

"What were you fighting about?"

I don't want her to get in trouble or anything. But I can't figure out how to say that without sounding stupid. *We're not supposed to talk.* No matter how you say it, it sounds whiny.

"It's not important anymore," I tell her.

Once you've noticed somebody's tits, it's hard to keep your eyes away from them. Tits are like magnets or something.

"Just out of curiosity, were you two fighting on the same side, or against each other?"

She's not stupid. Her mouth isn't quite smiling, but her eyes are. They're kind of a hazel color, but that's all I have time to notice before the magnetic field tries to take over. So I look over at Brandon. He's still staring down at his desk like he's ashamed or something.

12

What I can't figure out is why would anybody do anything they've got to be ashamed of later?

Still, it's not my job to rub his face in it. And now that I've made it clear how I feel about being hassled, I don't really care enough to *want* to rub his face in it.

"It's not important anymore," I say again.

Brandon's mouth is already turning into a bruise where I hit him. He flashes a look at me, like he's trying to tell me something—what, I couldn't say. He still won't look at Miss Rippen, but he seems to relax a little bit—he stretches out in his desk, like me.

Outside, it's sunny. You can tell it's hot as a mother, every bit as hot as it was when school started, back in the middle of August. It always seems hot in this place anyway, because the building's made from this pukey orange brick, and it's all rectangles surrounded by sidewalks and asphalt. Like a mid-sixties kind of thing.

It's kind of depressing, looking out the window, but there's not much going on in here, either. Brandon's working on math. I already finished mine— Trent's not the only one who makes good grades. Brandon's in the same advanced algebra class as me, but he probably doesn't even know it.

It's dead quiet. Mrs. Salinger's on duty now. I wish Miss Rippen was here, because there's nothing to do and maybe if she was here it would take my mind off how the silence is building up in my head.

I kind of start drawing in the margins of my math

paper. First I draw Miss Rippen, but her legs look all goofy, and I have to turn the paper in, so I erase Miss Rippen and doodle sports cars and stuff instead.

"I'm going to step out for a minute," Mrs. Salinger says.

Her voice is so loud after all that quiet, it's like she hit a gong or something. She fixes me and Brandon with that teacher look. You know, the evil eye.

"Just for one minute, and if either one of you moves or says a word, I'll make sure you regret it. Do you understand?"

She means it, but I know she'll be gone for more than a minute. The woman has some kind of problem. She spends half her life in the bathroom. They never should have put her in OCS, and if they knew she was leaving us in here alone, she'd be in a buttload of trouble. Which would be fine with me, I don't like her that much.

The door shuts behind her.

"You got a car, don't you?" I ask, just to shove away that awful buzzing quiet.

Brandon looks over at me, kind of surprised. Maybe because I have the nerve to speak to him and all. Or maybe because I knocked the crap out of him this morning—maybe I'm supposed to be his bitter enemy now or something. Like I care enough to hold a grudge.

But he puts his pencil down and stretches, like he's ready for a break in the quiet too. "Yeah."

"What kind?" Although I already know; I've seen it in the parking lot.

14

"Corvette."

I nod. It's silver. I would never drive it to school if I were him. I'd be afraid somebody might scratch it or something.

"I just got it. For my birthday," Brandon says.

"Sixteenth?"

"Yeah."

"I'll be sixteen this weekend."

"No kidding! My birthday was on the third. Hey, you getting a car?"

"No." I turn away and get busy looking out the window again.

I can't believe I have to spend the next three and a half days with this moron. Does he think everybody gets a car for their birthday?

For me, there's no point in even getting a license. Trent's always got our car, and if we could afford driver's ed, which we can't right now, we sure wouldn't be able to afford insurance.

"Hey," I hear Brandon say, "I didn't mean anything by that."

I'm thinking, Hell, he's so rich, he probably got *two* for his birthday. Matching cars, so the chauffeur can wash one while old Chase is getting the other one dirty.

It's kind of funny, and I smile to myself right before I blow the whole thing off. I look outside, at the sidewalks and asphalt, and try not to think about the silence. I can feel Chase watching me, but he doesn't say anything, and a few moments later I hear his pencil scratching again.

I still have my pencil in my hand. But I don't draw anything now. It seems kind of stupid to be drawing cars when the only other guy in the room got a brand-new Corvette for his birthday.

Almost as stupid as trying to talk to a guy who thinks everybody lives the same life he does.

— CHAPTER 3 —

Trent has to close the bookstore that night, so I don't get to talk to him until the next morning. There's not much to say. I tell him my version of what happened. Trent listens and nods and doesn't say much, but he can tell I'm telling the truth, and I can tell he's relieved I didn't get beat up. Neither one of us says anything about what he was really worried about.

See, a few years ago, back when Trent used to bring his friends home more, we started getting hang-up calls in the night. Then it got to where they'd say things before they hung up. The calls stopped about the time the guys in the apartment behind us got evicted, so we figured it must have been them.

The whole episode didn't last long, but it wasn't pleasant while it did last. And when your little brother's been woken up at three in the morning by somebody threatening to mutilate him, it kind of makes you tend to worry about things. Or at least it does Trent.

I'm not much of a worrier myself. When Trent

offers me a ride to school, I tell him no thanks, because then he'll be late. I just go on by myself. It's only a mile or so.

I walk into the OCS room right before the tardy bell. Brandon's already there, and he's already busy. I hear him say hi as I'm sitting down, but whoever he was talking to must have already passed by because I don't see anybody in the doorway or anything.

I get busy too. I try to work slow so I'll have something to do all day. I stop every once in a while and think about other stuff, so it'll last.

And during second period, I just pretend to work while I'm watching Miss Rippen. She's cutting things out of construction paper; like I said, she's a first-year teacher so she stills thinks she has to decorate the room and stuff. When she turns the scissors this way and that, her forehead kind of wrinkles up. She catches me watching her one time, and she just smiles at me. Even so, I start trying to look more busy, so she won't think I'm some kind of stalker or pervert or something.

Today she's wearing this pants-and-shirt kind of thing that's about as baggy and unappealing as you can get. But her hair's different; it's soft around her face today and when I ask her about one of my math problems, little wisps brush her cheek as she's bending over my book. She smells good, not like a department-store cologne counter, but like some kind of flower.

"I'm sorry, I never took advanced algebra," she says. "Strictly liberal arts. Brandon, you're in Charlie's class, aren't you? Don't you have the same assignment?"

"Uh, yeah," he says. Like he ever noticed I was in his class. And the thing is, I don't really need any help. I just wanted Miss Rippen to come lean over my desk.

"That's okay," I say, "I think I got it."

"You on fourteen?" Brandon asks.

"No, seventeen."

"What'd you get for fourteen?"

Like Miss Rippen isn't even in the room, like we're not supposed to be keeping perfectly quiet. What's he want to do, get her in trouble?

But Miss Rippen doesn't seem to mind.

"Pi over four," I tell him.

Brandon's frowning at his paper like, How the hell did *that* answer get on there?

"Charlie," Miss Rippen says, "why don't you show Brandon how you worked it? I don't think Ms. McGuiness would mind if you help each other. She wouldn't want one of you to fall behind."

Like I really want to help Richie Rich with his math. But I don't give a shit one way or the other, and the day's looming kind of long, and if Miss Rippen doesn't care if she gets fired, why should I? So I get up and take my book and paper over to Brandon's side of the room, and I show him how I worked the problem.

When I finish explaining, he says, "But shouldn't it be pi over two?" And damned if he isn't right. I canceled out on the top but not on the bottom.

"Shit," I say under my breath, and I erase the four and put a two. While I'm doing that, Brandon's working the problem out for himself, on his own paper. Not copying mine, but really working it, which I wouldn't have expected.

"The next one's kind of the same, isn't it?" he asks, looking at number fifteen.

"Yeah."

"Hang on, let me see what I get." So he does, and he gets the same answer I did.

Then the bell rings, and I figure I'd better get back in my seat before the next teacher takes over.

"Thanks," says Brandon.

He's a strange guy, that's for sure. Nice and friendly all of a sudden. Like he didn't notice what an asshole he was being till he got caught at it.

But Trent's the one who's good at figuring out all that psychological crap, not me, so I don't say you're welcome or anything.

Then Mr. Benton comes in, and Miss Rippen has to go her merry way. I wish she'd wear something besides that baggy outfit.

She does walk nice, though. From the back, the pants fit good, and her hips kind of swing from side to side.

As I'm leaning forward in my desk, watching her leave, I happen to catch Brandon's eye.

I look away real quick so I don't burst out laughing.

Because we're doing the exact same thing. I mean, we're both like stretched out on our desktops, about to tip over on our faces, watching Miss Rippen walk out of the room.

Even Mr. Benton is standing in the doorway craning his neck. God, it's funny. Things always seem hilarious when you're not supposed to be making any noise.

Out of the corner of my eye I see Brandon's shoulders shaking, so I know he's fighting it too. It reminds me of how my best friend Nick Andrade and I used to cut up in class sometimes.

But this is OCS, and Brandon isn't my friend. I slump back down in my seat. I hear Brandon stifle a snicker, but I don't look at him. I tug the smile back inside and open my French book. I try to ignore this tiny little part of me that's wishing I'd chosen Spanish instead.

I get busy studying the vocabulary words. I know that if I ignore it long enough, the little wishing part'll shut off all by itself.

CHAPTER 4

When school's out I start walking home like always. Our apartment is just inside the distance you have to live to ride the school bus.

When it's not raining and I don't have books to cart, like today, I kind of like walking. I think about things, and sometimes I even run, just for the hell of it. The thing is, I don't like to run in jeans. So I don't make a habit of running home from school.

I've just crossed Berry Street, which is like the main drag, when here comes this shining silver Corvette. I mean, the glare could kill me. Though I'd keep it up nice, too, if it was mine.

The Corvette pulls up and the tinted window comes buzzing down. "Hey, Calmont," says Brandon. "Want a ride?"

He's leaning over the passenger seat, but he's got on these mirror shades so I don't know if he's really looking at me or not, and my first thought is, He's going to drive me somewhere and beat the living daylights out of me. Or try.

But there's that car, and the window's down and I can see the dash, like something out of a space shuttle.

It'd almost be worth getting beat up, to ride in that car. Not that I've got anything to worry about. Brandon couldn't even get a punch in yesterday. And since then he's mostly had that puppy-wet-the-rug look.

These seats are leather. Leather, cool and sculpted-looking—they kind of surge up from the bottom of the car. The one on the passenger side's begging. *Charlie!* it says. *Slide your ass right over here!*

For once I don't give my head a chance to figure out what's best. I tuck myself in and next thing I know we're zooming along like we're on rails. I mean, low to the ground. The ride is actually a little on the bumpy side, which surprises me. You'd think it'd be smooth. I guess for smooth you need a luxury sedan or something.

"Where's your house?"

"Go this way," I say. I'm sniffing that new-car smell. It smells even better because of the leather seats.

Up ahead, I see this blond kid sitting on his trike at the end of his sidewalk. He's there every day, and I figure he must come out and wait for me, because every day he waves like a madman, going "Hi! Hi! Hi!" till I wave and say hi back. He's kind of a funny kid, but he seems all right, so when I see him up there on his red trike, I buzz down the window.

"Slow down," I tell Brandon, not even caring if he thinks I'm weird.

Brandon's looking all around. The kid's yard is full of junk, like old toys and rusted car parts. Brandon probably thinks I live here, but like I said, who cares what he thinks?

23

I wave and say "Hi," but the kid's just staring at me. Like he doesn't recognize me out of my natural habitat. Then, about the time I start the window back up, he figures it out. He gets this big old grin, like the sun just came out, and he's bouncing up and down all excited going "Hi! Hi! Hi!"

I settle back in my seat. I just hope the kid won't be disappointed tomorrow when I'm back on foot.

"Turn right up here," I tell Brandon. Now it occurs to me a car could probably get there faster going down Berry, but I've been cutting through this neighborhood so long I didn't think about that. It's not my gas we're wasting anyhow.

"You know that kid?" Brandon asks.

"No," I say. "Take a right around the circle and turn after the 7-Eleven. Man, this car is something else."

I didn't mean to say that last part. It just kind of came out. I mean, the stick shift doesn't even look like one; it looks like a place to rest your hand, like it grew out of the car instead of some assembly-line guy welding it there.

"Can you drive a standard?" I hear Brandon ask.

"Never tried," I tell him.

"Want to learn?"

He's nuts. He can't possibly be offering to let me drive his car.

I can't help it. "What do you mean?" I ask.

"Want me to show you?"

He doesn't even know me. Hell, a little over a day ago he was making fun of my shoes. Maybe he knows

24

he can't beat me up all by himself, and he wants to get me out where all his friends can jump me.

Or maybe it's the only way he knows to say he's sorry for ragging on me in the first place. By bribing me with his stupid car.

Well, it's working. "Sure."

Brandon turns back the way we came. I don't know where the hell he's taking me. We cross back over Berry, and the houses are different now. Closer to the high school they were mostly wood frame, some two-story, but mostly one; now they're older, with gables and stone porches.

"What's your dad do?" Brandon asks.

You don't make conversation with somebody you're about to ambush. I relax a little but not too much, because here comes the family history thing. "I'm not sure."

"You live with him?"

"No."

"Well, what's your mom do?"

I have to think about that one. Sometimes I get too literal, and I'm thinking, She doesn't do anything at all, except rot. "She's dead," I finally say.

"Oh. Sorry."

"It's okay," I say. These kinds of conversations make me uncomfortable, even after all these years. Maybe you never get used to it.

"So who do you live with?"

"My brother. He works in a bookstore," I say, to move things along.

"No kidding." He sounds interested and all, but

it could be part of that Leadership Committee thing, sounding interested when you don't really give a shit.

I don't ask him about his parents, and we end up in this parking lot at the edge of the college campus. It's mostly empty, because it's out by the stadium.

"This is where I learned to drive a standard," says Brandon.

I'm relieved he's not just going to switch places with me right in the middle of the street. I mean, I don't even have a learner's permit.

"I haven't taken driver's ed," I tell him, just in case he doesn't know.

"That's okay." The car's still running. He doesn't get out. "See these three pedals? This is the gas . . ."

No shit, I think.

"The one in the middle's the brake, and the one on the left is the clutch. The clutch is the important one."

I think the brake's pretty important too, but I let it go.

"You've got to push it in every time you change gears, or it'll strip 'em."

I can just see me stripping the gears on a rich guy's Corvette. God help me.

"The gears are set up like a double H," he says. "The middle is neutral. This"—he moves the stick shift around—"is first . . . second . . . third . . . fourth . . . fifth . . . and sixth."

I nod. I've got it.

"I'm putting it in neutral. See? Emergency

brake"—he pulls this handle—". . . on. Your turn."
And he's getting out of the car, which is still running.
I get out too, and we switch places.

I'm like a fighter pilot or something, strapping myself in, surrounded by all these buttons.

"Push the clutch in," he says, so I do. "Now try the
gears, so you know where they are."

First, second, third, fourth, fifth, sixth. Keeping the
clutch in.

"Now put it in first. Okay, release the brake. Now,
slowly, let off on the clutch while you're pushing the
gas."

I do. Nothing happens, except the engine keeps
getting louder and louder.

Just when I'm thinking I've done something
wrong, the whole car leaps forward and throws both
of us back in our seats like we're in some NASA grav-
ity experiment.

Except now the car's moving, and I don't know
what to do.

"Shit!" I say.

We're going faster and faster. The engine's getting
loud again. I've got to turn now so we don't jump the
curb, but I can't think how to brake if I've got to keep
my foot free for the clutch. We take the turn a little
too sharp.

"Second gear," Brandon says, so I push the clutch
in with my foot and shift into second. Another lurch,
and then the engine sounds happier. Quieter.

"It takes a while to get used to the play in the
clutch," he says. "Stop, and try starting again."

So I put my right foot on the brake, and we're slowing, very smoothly.

Good deal, I think.

That's when the whole car makes this horrible coughing sound and starts flinging us back and forth like it's a bucking bronco or something.

"Clutch in! Clutch in!" Brandon's yelling, and by God, I get that clutch in, once I find it. "Use the clutch when you're about to stop, too."

"Clutch. Stop. Got it." My face feels kind of hot.

"Don't worry. I got a couple of neck braces in the trunk," Brandon says, but he's grinning.

"Aw, shut up," I say, like I do to Trent.

After a few go-rounds I actually get up to fourth gear, and Brandon asks if I want to try driving back to my place, but I tell him no thanks. I'm doing okay, but it might get tricky out where there's other cars.

"Left, to South Hills, then right," I tell Brandon, once we're rolling. Man, he drives smooth. I didn't appreciate it before. No jerks, and the engine always sounds happy. Old Chase knows how to keep a happy engine.

On the way back, I'm thinking how on Monday this guy was on my case, and today he's letting me drive his car. *This* car. He doesn't even seem scared I'll wreck it or something. And I can't think of any way to ask him about it that doesn't sound stupid.

But I really want to know, so I figure, Tough shit.

"What's the deal?" I ask. "Yesterday you're an asshole, and today you're giving out free driving lessons."

He shifts gears like he doesn't even have to think about where his foot is. "I don't know. You were pretty cool about what happened, and we didn't have any business messing with you like that. I just kind of felt bad," he says. "And you're kind of an asshole yourself. Sitting in *my* car calling *me* an asshole."

I swear to God he sounds like Trent. The way he just discusses instead of getting mad. And then nails you with a word.

I can't help but almost smile. I'm thinking, though, that Trent wouldn't have called me an asshole. Nick would've, but not Trent.

Brandon kind of shakes his head to himself; he *is* smiling, under those mirrored shades.

"You don't let anything get to you, do you?" he asks.

"No." I can see the apartments up ahead. "What's the point?" I'm kind of wishing there was somebody waiting for me there, inside. Anybody, to break the silence.

"No point, I guess. It's just hard not to, sometimes."

This is where I should say something like "What's the fastest you've ever taken this thing?" or even just "Yeah." But I almost feel like I'm sitting here with Trent or Nick, so I say, "Like what?"

"I don't know. Like keeping on top of stuff."

I start to ask on top of what stuff, but I think maybe he means on top of school stuff. Like being on the LC and all that. Maybe he means he has to worry about keeping his rep among his friends.

"Turn in at those apartments," I tell him.

Because I'm not really interested in some sob story about how he didn't wear the right socks one day and got reamed over by his buddies. Boo-hoo.

I tell him how to go through the parking lot to get to my apartment. Then I'm like, "Thanks," and I'm getting out of the car. It's so low-slung it's like climbing out of a cocoon.

"See you tomorrow," he says.

"Yeah." I swing the door shut and walk off. Brandon revs up and I hear him going, but I don't look. I'd like to watch that car take those corners, but I'll be damned if I'm going to stand there and stare after it. And I've practically forgotten I was on the verge of inviting him in.

It's Tuesday, so Trent probably won't be home until after six. I'm walking up the apartment stairs, and they're making this awful echoey metal sound. It's a very lonely sound, like thousands of people have tromped up and down these stairs and never left a footprint or even a scuff. Nobody stays for long in apartments. Except me and Trent; we've been here six years, like I said. And Nick, my best friend, he was here for almost that long. That's a long time in one apartment.

But most people in apartments never bother to get to know each other. And that's what metal stairs sound like.

I unlock the door and walk in. We keep the place pretty clean, considering we're two guys living alone. I mean, our furniture's about a thousand years old and all, but there's no pizza crusts on the floor or anything.

I'm thinking about Nick today, which I seldom do because, what's the point? But today I just feel like it. Nick's one of the few people I ever trusted. One of two, I guess, and the other one's Trent.

When Nick was here, we'd always be doing something after school. We'd play hockey in the parking lot or basketball at the middle school across the street. When we were kids we'd go down to the creek by the soccer fields and goof around, wading and throwing rocks and trying to catch minnows. As we got older we'd go jogging around the fields, then walk along the creek to cool off. Sometimes we'd talk about stuff. Nothing important, just girls, movies, whatever.

But this summer Nick's mom got remarried and they had to move to Phoenix. Nick and I don't write or call or anything. It wouldn't be the same.

Still, it hits me how I miss laughing and messing around with somebody. Somebody you don't even have to tell stuff to, because they already know what you're thinking anyway. I mean, Trent and I get along real well and all, but he's twenty-four and in college, and he doesn't think about girls the way I do.

I'm kind of hungry, so I grab a bag of chips and lean against the counter, eating them in the kitchen. But it's too quiet. I can't stand it. I hate quiet. So I go sit on the couch and turn on the TV and start eating my chips there. But all that's on are reruns and talk shows, and it's like, I'm not *that* desperate, am I?

What the hell kind of life is this? Stale chips out of a bag and *Oprah*.

I'm looking at the phone, and it occurs to me I could call Megan. Boy, would that keep me occupied.

And that's how desperate I am. Thinking for even a split second about calling some girl it's taken me a month to get rid of. It'd probably take me another month to get rid of her again, if I call her just once.

I chuck the chips back in the pantry and change clothes to go jogging. By myself.

My mind clears out when I'm running, it always does, but when I've finished, when I'm cooling down, I happen to walk by the apartment swimming pool and I think maybe I won't go back up just yet.

Nobody's around, even though it's only the first week of September and it's still hot. I start to take off my shoes and socks so I can go sit on the side of the pool. The thing is, I don't have a towel and I know if I stick even a toe in, I'll end up swimming, and I don't really feel like swimming today.

So I end up sitting on the end of one of the lounges, watching the water. I like water. To look at, I mean. Most people just look at it and see water, but I see movement and light—I mean, it's more alive than people are, because most people are all surface, but water's always surface and depth. And water takes on the shape of whatever it's in, like a glass or a pool or a bathtub. I can usually get peaceful, just looking at it.

But today, I'm sitting here and I'm thinking, What a sad life you have, Charlie. You don't make an effort to get to know anybody. Like being a little bit friendly's going to kill you. No wonder you're here by yourself.

Long before she died, my mom shut herself up and stopped going out. That was when we lived in East Texas. And kids at school would invite themselves over, like you do when you're in first or second grade. And I'd have to tell them no, because you never knew what shape my mom would be in. I just kept saying no, until finally nobody asked anymore.

When you're a kid, there's a little knot that gets going in your stomach. It only comes when what *has* to happen and what you *wish* could happen are two different things.

It was always real quiet in our old house in East Texas, because Trent and I never brought our friends home. That's why I can't stand silence now.

And that's why I'm thinking maybe I should have invited Brandon up, even if he does think everybody gets a car for their birthday. Because now that Nick's not here, I'm on the edge of getting comfortable with being alone.

Because, looking at the water, it hits me that if I'm not careful, I'll take on the shape of my mom.

CHAPTER 5

Lunch is pretty awful in OCS. Coach Wills comes to walk us down to the cafeteria between lunches, and we're the only three people in there. We go through the line, and Brandon gets to watch me pay for my lunch with a card while he pulls out real cash. It's probably torture or something for him to eat cafeteria food. Sophomores aren't supposed to eat lunch off campus, but a lot of them do. If they're like Brandon, the leaders of the community and all, nobody's going to hassle them for a little thing like eating lunch off campus.

On Wednesday we get our stuff and sit down, leaving two chairs between us like we're supposed to, and Coach Wills relaxes with the business section of the paper like he has for the past three days.

So we're sitting there in this huge old cavern of a cafeteria, and I'm trying to cut into this rubbery steak stuff that's probably been sitting out since first lunch. I notice that Brandon's not even trying. I wouldn't eat it either, but I'm hungry. I finally get a bite sawed loose, when I hear this voice that almost makes me spit it back out.

"Coach Wills?" It's Luke Cottington, all helpful. "Mrs. Angelino said to tell you the Ad building's on line four."

"Figures," Coach Wills mutters to himself. He eyes me and Chase. I try out the green beans. "I guess I can count on you two not to rob the cafeteria ladies, right?" He folds up the paper and lays it on the table. "I'll be back in two shakes. Chase, you move and I'll kill you. What's your name?"

He's looking at me.

"Charlie Calmont," I say.

"Calmont, you move and I'll kill you too. Ask Chase. Chase, will I kill him if he moves?"

"He'll kill you if you move," Brandon tells me.

"Cottington, get the hell back to wherever you're supposed to be," Coach Wills says, like Luke's some fly that's buzzing around. Then he heads out the door, not bothering to check if we're doing what he told us to do.

The minute he disappears, Luke takes Coach's chair, turns it around, and straddles it, grinning at Brandon.

"Hey, Chase. Haven't heard from you. How's prison life?"

"I thought y'all had a test or something, fourth," Brandon says.

"I finished. Mr. Hammond asked me to take some stuff to the office."

So now Cottington's got his hands on a hall pass. Mr. Hammond'll be lucky to see him again before the bell rings.

35

But it's got nothing to do with me, so I just start in on my mashed potatoes.

"What'd your parents say about you getting busted?" Cottington asks.

Out of the corner of my eye I see Brandon shrug.

"That bad, huh?" Cottington looks around. "I'm surprised Coach didn't chain you to the wall. You're the type that'll tunnel out, if you get a chance."

"Get out of here, man," Brandon says. "He'll be back any minute."

"What's the matter, you afraid they'll put you in solitary?"

"Talk about being afraid," I say through a mouthful of roll. That's the only thing you can count on always being decent in a cafeteria, the rolls.

Cottington's been ignoring me, but now he kind of has to notice me. "What the fuck is that supposed to mean?"

Brandon's been poking at his food with a fork, but now he glances at me and puts it down. "I think," he says to Cottington, "it means you started the whole thing and then disappeared when they started hauling us in."

I don't say anything now, because I don't know why I butted into their conversation in the first place. But I'm enjoying the way Cottington's face looks, like maybe he's been put on the outside looking in, but he's not sure.

"I got to get going," he says after a minute, getting up from Coach's chair. "See you around."

"See you," says Brandon, real friendly.

"See you," I say for no particular reason. Cottington doesn't answer. He just leaves.

Coach Wills comes in, but he's standing in the cafeteria doorway hollering at somebody just out of sight. Brandon's trying to get interested in his lunch tray.

I like how he knew what I was talking about, and I like the way he told Cottington off.

"You ever play street hockey?" I ask Brandon in a low voice, keeping an eye on Coach Wills in the doorway.

"Yeah."

Now my head's wondering what the hell my mouth's doing. "Want to come over after school?" it's asking Brandon. "There's this corner of the parking lot where Nick Andrade and I used to play all the time. It's pretty decent."

He doesn't answer right away, and it's pretty obvious he's got some problem with it. Which my head is thinking may be good.

I scrape the last of the mashed potatoes off my plate. This stupid little knot's trying to get started in the middle of my stomach, but I give it a kick and tell it to get the hell out. If he does, he does; if he doesn't, he doesn't. No skin off my ass, either way.

"Yeah, okay." Whatever the problem was, he's blown it off. But I'm still a little pissed at myself, at my mouth for asking, and at the rest of me for almost giving a shit what he answered.

Then Coach comes back over and we've got to do the silence thing again. The stupid thing is, on top of being pissed, I actually feel kind of light. Like I just finished a ten-mile run or something.

When the last bell rings, Brandon waits for me to collect my stuff, and we walk out of OCS together. It's only like two doors down from the outside exit, but we still pass about a million people, and they're all saying "Hi, Brandon" and "Hey, Chase." I feel like I'm with a politician or something. I don't say anything, and except for "Hi," neither does Brandon, until we're heading toward the parking lot.

"Cottington can be a real asshole," he tells me right out of the blue.

It kind of surprises me. That he knows Cottington's an asshole. And that he'd admit it like that. "So why do you hang out with him?"

"He's all right sometimes. He knows how to have fun."

"How do you have fun?" I ask while he's unlocking his door. I'm wondering what fun is to someone like Cottington. Maybe kicking dogs, or spitting off bridges.

"How do you think? Get wasted."

We get in his car, and I don't say anything. I don't have anything against drinking, in fact I don't have anything against getting drunk. It doesn't bother me like you might think, considering my mom and all.

The thing that bothers me about it is, drinking's the criterion for fun?

The reason I say that, is because my mom died

from it. She finally got to where she wouldn't even eat anymore; she just drank. I remember how she was dying, and she just kept getting more and more yellow until even the whites of her eyes were yellow, and the whole house started smelling like death, even though she wasn't dead. And then they came and took her to the hospital and she died there.

Drinking's okay, like I say. I just don't like it when people think it's the only thing there is in the world. It almost scares me when people act like that, to tell the truth.

"So the only time he's not an asshole is when he's drunk," I say, and then I realize we're practically at the apartment and Brandon was in the middle of some sentence when I interrupted him. Brandon's a talker, I guess.

There's this moment while Brandon's trying to figure out what the hell I'm talking about.

"Yeah," he finally says. Pretty polite, considering.

"Pull in here," I tell him. "So why do you hang around with him when he's *not* drunk?"

"Hell if I know. Force of habit, I guess."

We get out of the car, and I lead the way up the stairs. There's nothing more to say, but I'm thinking maybe Brandon is like water, maybe he takes on the shape of whoever he's with. And maybe he knows it, and he's trying not to be that way anymore. Which is kind of brave, if you think about it.

There's a moment of confusion where Brandon thinks you have to play street hockey on Rollerblades, and I have to tell him that not all of us *have* Rollerblades. What I do have is my hockey stick, and Nick's, because his mom made him get rid of it when he busted the window of a car, and a puck, and chalk to mark the goals on the curbs.

The heat's rising off the pavement, and I can hear air-conditioning units kicking on as we walk down to the parking lot. Then we face off, and the world narrows to getting hold of the puck and slamming it between the chalk lines. All I hear is the slapping and scraping of sticks. That, and Brandon being his own announcer whenever he scores.

We have to stop every once in a while for a car, but we're pretty evenly matched, and I forget about moms and shit like that. It's been a while since I had anybody to do stuff with.

"And Calmont makes the steal," Brandon's saying as I get the puck and head for the goal. We've been playing long enough that my shirt's sticking to me, long enough that it must be getting close to dinner because we have to stop for cars more frequently. "He takes the shot, and . . . scores!" He started being my announcer, too, a while back. I don't care. I think it's kind of funny.

"Hey, Charlie!"

It's Trent, in his car. Thursday's one of his days off from work but he usually spends it on campus, studying and working out at the P.E. building after class. "What's for dinner?" he's yelling at me.

"Don't ask me!" I yell back. "He thinks he's Mr. Brady and I'm Alice the maid," I tell Brandon as Trent pulls into a parking spot.

40

"I guess I oughta go now," Brandon says, but he doesn't seem too thrilled with the idea. He's not the announcer anymore, he just stands there picking at an old piece of tape on Nick's hockey stick.

"You can eat here, if you don't mind fish sticks or something," I tell him, grabbing our stuff. I know Trent won't care. In fact, he'll be relieved I'm having contact with another human being. He thinks it's his fault I'm not some social butterfly.

Brandon shrugs. "I don't mind." He doesn't say a word about checking with his parents. Maybe they don't care either.

We're both sweating like pigs as we head over to Trent. "Hey," I greet him.

"Hey." He's getting his backpack. It's loaded. He's always got stuff to do.

"This is Brandon. He's going to eat with us."

"Okay. Hi, Brandon."

On the way through the complex Brandon's smiling to himself.

"What's so funny?" I ask.

"By now my mom would know your family history and your G.P.A. And my dad would be telling you what sports you ought to play."

"Remind me to bring my résumé, if I ever go to your house," I say.

Brandon gives this little laugh. "Don't worry. I'll try to spare you."

"Who won?" asks Trent as we head up the stairs.

"I don't know," I tell him.

"You did," Brandon says. "Twelve to ten."

41

It's nice and cool inside. I take the hockey sticks from Brandon and throw them in my room. He's smiling again, but I don't know why.

"Looks like fish sticks," says Trent, who's got his head in the freezer.

"Told you," I say to Brandon.

Dinner ends up being fish sticks, canned black-eyed peas, and canned corn. Not too different from cafeteria food, really. Brandon's eating all right, but he's not saying much.

"So," Trent says, "You're the one with the Corvette?"

"Yes," says Brandon.

"What's the fastest you've ever taken it?"

"I'm not sure."

Trent and I look at each other.

"He's not a cop," I tell Brandon.

"Maybe seventy-five, eighty."

"Yeah, right," I say through a mouthful of corn.

Brandon eyes me, and then Trent. "A hundred and ten," he says very clearly.

Trent nods. He shoves a bowl at Brandon. "More peas?"

A smile flickers over Brandon's face. "Thanks." He spoons himself a second helping. He doesn't seem to care that we don't eat gourmet food or anything. "Charlie said you work at a bookstore," he tells Trent.

"Yeah."

"You like it?"

"Most of the time. Anything'll get monotonous after a while, I guess. Hey, Charlie, I didn't tell you. We got Travis Modine coming for an autographing."

"No kidding."

"Who's Travis Modine?" Brandon asks.

"He's a singer," I tell him.

"No," corrects Trent, "he's a *country* singer, which is not the same thing. A country singer who paid some poor slob to ghostwrite his autobiography."

"You like country?" Brandon asks me, and the look on his face is like I just admitted I've got a thing for goats or something.

"Yeah, so?"

Trent's laughing. "See, Charlie? I'm not the only one around here with some taste."

"Hey," I tell him. "At least country lyrics have a little *meaning*."

"And melodies stolen from rock. Right, Brandon?"

"I don't listen to it much."

"If you lived here you would," Trent says. "Against your will. It's like a nightmare where you can never wake up."

"You don't look like the country type," Brandon says to me.

"He left his boots under the bed," Trent sings as he gets up and starts clearing his plate. *"Nair nair."*

"Jeez," I say, "will you guys lay off?" Although Brandon hasn't said all that much.

But I notice he's actually eaten all his food. More than he's eaten in the cafeteria this whole week.

"This place is so different from my house," he tells me while Trent's in the kitchen.

"How?" I ask, thinking, Do I want some more fish sticks or not? There's a few left.

"My dad always picks a topic and we have to talk about it. Like a current event or something. It's like writing a report."

His family's starting to sound like a pain in the ass. "Sounds exciting," I tell him. No, I'll save the fish sticks for tomorrow. I like cold fish sticks.

"Speaking of dads," Trent calls from the sink. "Do your parents know you're eating over here?"

"No," says Brandon. "I guess I'd better call."

"Now that it's too late," says Trent.

Brandon just smiles.

"Phone's over there," I tell him. I pick up his plate and mine, and take them into the kitchen.

Brandon picks up the phone and dials.

"Hey, Marina. I need to talk to my mother. Mom? At a friend's house. Charlie. Calmont. I know, but . . . kind of; his brother's here. Yes, I hear you. Can we talk about this la— . . . What do you want, a . . . Fine. Yeah. Yes *ma'am*."

Click. "Stupid bitch," Brandon mutters.

I figure Marina must be the maid or something.

"I've got to go," Brandon says, heading for the door. "Thanks for dinner."

"Anytime," I say.

"No, really, man," says Brandon, like this was some big deal or something. "Thanks."

As the door shuts behind him, I'm pretty sure of one thing. I'm not the only one who doesn't like to go home.

CHAPTER 6

Thursday is our last day of OCS, and boy, does it drag. The closest thing to a high point comes during second period, when Brandon calls Miss Rippen over to his desk. She's wearing jeans, which is weird because usually teachers only wear jeans on Fridays. And her jeans aren't those pouchy things all the other teachers wear. They fit good.

Anyway, she's bending over talking to him, so I set my pencil down to observe a moment of Ass Appreciation. And that's about as thrilling as my day gets.

I won't miss OCS, but I'm sure going to miss Miss Rippen.

When the bell rings, at the end of sixth, I head for the door. Brandon's slowly getting up from his desk. "Hey," he says, and I stop. "You going to the game tomorrow night?"

"No." I actually paid once to go to a football game. Nobody else watched it. Everyone just stood, for the whole entire game, talking. Like they didn't see each other all day in school.

"Guess I'll see you around then," he tells me. I can

45

see David Carlson through the little window in the door. Maybe he's waiting for Chase.

I figure "guess I'll see you around" is Brandon's way of saying "it's been real, but now I've got to go hang with my friends." Which is fine with me, I didn't sign up to be his buddy or anything.

"Yeah." I look right at him and nod, like I do with Trent. It's like a handshake, we're in agreement: no hard feelings, but the convention's over—time to get back to real life.

I reach for the doorknob. "Hey," he says again. I look at him, and he's busy putting all this stuff in his backpack. "Want a ride home?" he asks without looking up.

I don't answer right away. I'm thinking.

"Why?" I finally ask.

He shrugs. "It's been raining," he says, zipping his backpack. "And you're all right," he adds as he slings it over his shoulder. "And I'm tired of being around people who're always looking for a reason to jump my case."

I guess he means Cottington. Cottington's supposed to be his friend, but look how he was jerking his chain in the cafeteria.

"Okay," I tell him, meaning he can give me a ride home. What the hell, right? Ride in the Corvette?

"Oh, thank you," he says, kind of sarcastic, but he's grinning. "Ready?"

"Yeah."

* * *

46

So we're walking across the rich people's parking lot. It's the only parking lot with trees, so I guess that's why they claimed it. Or maybe because it's by the field house, and so many of them are involved with the football team in one way or another.

It's been raining off and on all day, but it's clearing up a little now, and the temperature's dropped enough that it feels good—it's that first cool day in September. I'm taking it in, sniffing the air, checking out how everything looks green and happy.

"Hey, Chase," calls Luke. He's with a few other people, sitting on the hood of somebody's car. That's the only drawback to a day like this—the metal's not hot enough to burn Cottington's ass. "What's up?" he asks.

"Not much," says Brandon.

"Oh boy," says Luke, glancing at me. "Going to play some more *games?*"

I can't stand him, the way he says things all loud and sarcastic, like he's got to entertain everybody.

"Maybe," says Brandon, and he gives Luke this look like, Got a problem with that?

"If you get tired of hockey, you could try Candy Land."

I'd love to knock the crap out of him. I'd love to see him lying on the ground looking up at me, so surprised and scared he can't think of anything to say for once.

"What's so funny?" Brandon asks me over the roof of his car, and I realize I'm kind of smiling at the mental picture I'm getting.

"Nothing," I tell him. Cottington's his friend, right? At least when he's drunk, he is.

"I'll tell you a theory I have," Brandon says after we're in the car, heading down Berry Street. Windows rolled down, of course. "But it's just a theory, so don't say anything to anybody."

"Okay," I say. I don't know anybody to say anything to, and I'm just enjoying being in the Corvette again.

"Cottington's been going out with this girl. Nobody's said anything to me, but I've seen her looking at you. I was thinking maybe she kind of likes *you,* and Cottington knows it. You know what I'm saying?"

"I guess." I'm almost wondering who the hell he's talking about, but that's all I need, some girl liking me. I've been down that road, and it's a royal pain— first they're all happy you're just talking to them, and about two seconds later they're expecting you to give them your heart on a platter or something.

So I blow it off. It's just a theory anyway. I mean, Cottington's like a baseball star and he's got buttloads of bucks. And of course, I don't have the right shoes.

Brandon seems like he's waiting for me to say something else. When I don't, he starts messing with the radio, trying to find something he likes. For just a second "Adalida," by George Strait, comes through the speakers. Loud.

"So you like this stuff, huh?" Brandon asks, tuning it in better. "Hey, I know this. Didn't it used to be a beer commercial?"

"Yeah," I say.

He listens for a minute. "It's not too bad. Maybe because it reminds me of beer."

"Could be," I say.

"I guess I kind of like it," he admits. "What station is this?"

"Sounds like KSCS," I tell him.

"It's pretty catchy," Brandon says, and then we're stopping for a red light at the intersection of University and Berry. To the right is the college. To the left are apartments and houses.

This Jeep pulls up beside us, in the left-turn lane. The driver looks like a college girl. She has blond hair, long, pulled back in a ponytail. Her legs are long, too, and tan, in denim shorts. She smiles at us. I don't know about Brandon, but I kind of smile back.

"Aaaaaaaaaaadalida," George Strait is singing. The fiddles are practically bouncing out of the speakers.

Brandon reaches down. His fingers fumble at a dial, and the song kind of goes away.

That's when it hits me. He's turning it down so this girl won't think he listens to country music.

But didn't he just say he liked this song? It almost bugs me. Almost. Enough that I'm not thinking about the girl's long legs anymore.

I tell myself it's none of my business if the guy's afraid of what people think. If he's a wuss.

Brandon glances at me. "What?" he asks.

Usually I don't let my face show much. Usually I keep it pretty still. But today, here, with Brandon, my face feels like it might be saying what I'm thinking, loud and clear: What a wuss.

Brandon looks away. He drums his fingers on the steering wheel. He looks up and checks the traffic light. It's still red.

"Okay," he says, not looking at me or the girl. And he turns the radio back on. Loud. His face is like stone. Like he actually thinks this girl might laugh at him. Like she even cares what he listens to.

The left-turn arrow flashes, and before Brandon can check the girl's reaction, she's pulling out. As her Jeep turns, we both crane our necks to watch. And there, on her back bumper, we see a sticker with large red-and-black letters: KSCS 96.3.

I can't help it, I laugh.

Brandon's just sitting there. Then he cracks a little smile, like, joke's on him. But all he says is: "Aw, shut up."

We're zipping around the curve that leads past the soccer fields.

"You like vodka?" he asks.

"It's all right," I say.

"I've got a bottle at home," Brandon tells me. "We could get it and go down to the park."

"What park?"

"There's one by my house."

I'm thinking about the silence that's waiting for me, and those metal stairs. About how I don't have to drink much if I don't want to.

"Okay," I tell him.

So we go straight instead of turning toward the apartments, and we go down a hill to this neighborhood where each house is about a block long and there are trees all over the place. I mean, it's like a forest.

Brandon's house is a big old sprawling thing with fake wooden shutters. We pull up into the garage, and I notice no one else seems to be home.

From the inside, the house is even more sprawling. It's got like a million living rooms or something, and that's just on the way to Brandon's bedroom.

His room is about as big as our whole apartment. There's even a step up to the part where his bed is. The whole thing is color coordinated and spotless. It looks like a picture out of a magazine.

But something about it doesn't seem right. Not lived in. I mean, in a magazine, they'll always put in some little bit of fake disorder, like an open book on a table, or a plate of food, all artistically arranged. Because they think that'll make it look like people really live there.

But in Brandon's room, there's no books, and no food.

"Welcome to the museum," Brandon says while he's walking over to a door, and when he opens it, I see that it's a closet.

"You don't like it?" I mean, it's his room, after all.

"No." He pulls this metal box out from the back. It's the kind of thing you'd keep files in, with a combination lock on it, and he opens it. Inside, there aren't any files, just papers and stuff that I don't get a good look at, and a bottle.

"So why do you keep it this way if you don't like it?"

"I don't." He takes out the bottle and shuts the box again. "Ready?"

"Yeah."

I don't particularly want to drink straight vodka, but I'm thinking it might be rude to go to somebody's house and tell them how to fix your drink.

"Screwdrivers okay with you?" Brandon asks, and I'm kind of relieved.

If you can believe it, we end up pouring vodka and orange juice into two sports bottles. Because it's broad daylight, and we're going to the park.

It's just down the hill from his house, next to a tiny creek, and you can tell what kind of park it is. I mean, some of the other parks have broken glass and graffiti all over the place. This one is cleaned up. There's no crap clogging up the creek, either. It's the same with the streets over here—no potholes. When you live in this part of town, you can make the city keep things up, I guess.

There's a couple of moms with their little kids, and everybody has on matching clothes and hair ribbons and shoes and stuff. It reminds me of the little kid on his trike, in his yard full of junk. Does his mom ever take him to the park? Does he even have a mom? I've never seen any mom or dad, just the kid all alone at the end of the sidewalk.

We go off to sit on top of a picnic table, kind of

away from the moms and kids. There's these huge trees all around.

I pull the little cap off the straw and take a couple of sips. There's a basketball court nearby, and I wish I had a basketball so we could play. I used to have one, but it got a leak in it.

"You got a basketball?" I ask, because actually I'd rather be playing basketball than drinking.

"At home," says Brandon. He's chugging the vodka, which is pretty stupid.

"If you puke, don't expect me to clean it up," I tell him.

"Don't worry. I never get sick."

"How often do you do this?" I ask. I mean, is this guy a lush, or what?

"Weekends, mostly."

"That's pretty sad," I say without thinking. Then I'm kind of sorry, because it's rude even if it's true.

Brandon shrugs. "What else is there to do?"

"You could play basketball, for one thing. Or go to a movie. Go pick up girls. I don't know."

"All of which are more fun if you're drunk."

Even sadder, but I don't say anything this time.

"What are you, anyway," he asks me, "the recruiter for AA?"

"No, my mother drank herself to death."

I take a big sip out of my sports bottle, because I shouldn't have said that. I just wanted to make him shut up. I don't like anybody expecting things out of me—like there's some kind of yardstick, and if you don't measure up, you're a loser.

Brandon's looking at me. Like he's trying to decide if I'm just messing with him.

I notice the moms and kids are heading off. I guess they're all suburban buddies who came together.

"You're not kidding, are you?" he asks.

"Nope."

"But where's your dad?"

"I don't know. He and my mom got divorced when I was real little."

"Do you have any grandparents, or uncles or aunts?"

"No."

"So your brother's like your only family?" Brandon's forgotten about his drink, and I can see him kind of feeling sorry for me.

"Trent always took care of me, even when my mom was alive. The truth is, I was kind of relieved she was gone," I tell him.

"Man."

Like I'm some kind of freak story. Like I should be on *Oprah* or something. From what I heard on the phone, he doesn't get along with *his* mom too well.

"So, what's the deal with your room?" I ask.

Brandon remembers his drink all of a sudden. I'm thinking he's not going to answer.

"It's not my room," he says after a minute. "It's my parents' room—they just let me live there. They fixed it the way they like, and I keep it according to specifications."

He spits all this out like it tastes bad. He sounds different, bitter. This is not the guy who made fake crowd sounds every time he scored in hockey yesterday.

And it must be pretty bad at home if he's got to lock up papers so nobody reads them. I couldn't tell you the last time Trent was in my room.

"You got a nice house, though," I tell him.

"Yeah. Real nice."

I watch him chug a little more, and I'm thinking, This is one unhappy guy. I actually kind of feel sorry for him. I remember Brandon's face smiling out of all those posters at Leadership Committee election time, till you were sick of seeing them. But that was paper taped to a wall, and this is real.

And he's stuck with friends like Cottington, who thinks unhappy means you've got to go to the store for another six-pack.

Poor old Chase. He's like real, or trying to be, and he's stuck in this color-coordinated house in this color-coordinated neighborhood with these color-coordinated friends who rag on anybody who plays a sport without lining up in uniform. No wonder he's chugging.

"Hey," I say.

He's leaning over, kind of moody, playing with his straw.

"Forget this shit. Let's go get your basketball. One-on-one."

Brandon looks at me. He's obviously thinking something, but who the hell knows what it is? Maybe how he ought to humor me on account of my dead mother. Maybe how sad he looks to somebody like me. Maybe how boring it is to get blasted every week-end. Who knows?

"All right," he says.

We go get his basketball, and we end up dumping the screwdrivers down the sink at his house, and Brandon gripes a little about the waste, but what else can we do with them? Back at the park it turns out he's not bad, but he tries to get too fancy. So I can steal the ball while he's dribbling all over the place like a maniac.

While we're playing, I notice these two girls coming along the bike trail. They're like JV cheerleaders or something. I don't go to football games, like I said. So I think these girls are cheerleaders, but I'm not sure. They're not wearing their uniforms.

They slow down as they pass. And then they stop, right in the middle of the bike trail—they're really giving us the once-over. I took my shirt off a while back because it's hot, and I'm thinking I'm kind of glad I've been working out with Trent some.

So I start getting a little fancy too. We're like the Harlem Globetrotters or something.

And then we're feeling kind of thirsty, so we go over to the stone drinking fountain that's a little closer to the trail. We're standing there, drinking and horsing around. But the girls don't come over. Finally, they just get on their bikes and leave.

"The one in the blue shorts is Autumn Marquette," Brandon says, spinning the basketball in his hands as he looks after them. "Luke says he did her after the Southern Hills game." Autumn and her friend are disappearing around a bend. "Luke's a goddamn liar."

"How do you know?" I ask. Although I agree, Luke is a liar. He looks like a liar.

"He can't get his story straight. One time it was in the car, another time it was at her parents' house."

Miss Rippen pops into my head. I wonder if she has a boyfriend. If she has an apartment, or where she lives. Where she does it. If she does.

"So," Brandon asks, spinning the basketball some more, "did you ever do it?"

"Yeah," I say. But that's all I say.

"Who?"

I don't answer right away. I'm thinking if it's any of his business or not. But you know, you can't shut yourself up in a box and never trust anybody, and this isn't like a major detail or anything.

"Megan Dunlop," I tell him.

He tucks the ball under his arm. "You're kidding."

"Nope."

"She's a junior." He's looking at me, like now he's got to reevaluate or something.

"Yeah."

"And she's so *quiet.*"

Well, she's not always quiet, but I'm not going to tell him that. Megan's okay, you know.

"You?" I ask.

"Yeah." He hesitates. "Well, kind of."

"Kind of?"

Brandon gets this pained look. "We were like right in the middle of it, I mean, I was just getting it in, and her parents came home."

"Aw, man," I say. You got to feel for him. Talk about frustrating. "So what happened?"

"It's kind of funny, now. There they are, coming in the front door, flipping on lights, and we're back in the den trying to get all our clothes on—"

"Now, who was this?" I interrupt.

"Carly Drake. I'm like hopping around to get my pants zipped and she gets her skirt all pulled down, and they come in and we're like sitting watching TV, and she says, 'Oh, hi, Mom. Hi, Dad.' "

He says this in a Carly Drake voice. I start smiling.

"And her mom says, 'Don't you need a little more *light*?' And she hits the switch and all of a sudden I see Carly's bra on the floor. So I like put my foot on it and shove it under the couch."

I'm trying not to laugh, but I can't help it.

"And her dad's giving me the evil eye, but I can't get up because I've still got this huge boner."

By now Brandon's laughing too, although I bet he sure wasn't laughing when it happened.

"So I look right at him, and with this straight face, I say, 'How was the movie, Mr. Drake?' After that, her dad won't let her go out with me." Brandon's smile is kind of falling. "He tells her no car dates, either."

And now he's got to see her at school all the time. Poor guy. Once you've seen a girl naked, it's like engraved in your brain, no matter how many clothes she wears.

"Her dad's a real bastard." Brandon shakes his head. "So, how was Megan?"

I hold my hands up, like, Hand me the ball. He tosses it to me. "Pretty good."

"You just do it once?"

"No." I start walking up and down, passing the ball behind me, messing around.

"So were you, like, dating or something?"

"She *thought* we were." I shoot the ball at his chest. *Whump!* He catches it, solid. "Now she doesn't."

That sounds awful. Cold. But it's true. When I found out she thought it meant more than it did, I quit seeing her. What else could I do? Keep porking her, which would make her think I cared? Not me.

I pick up the ball and bounce it a few times on the concrete. "You know who I wouldn't mind doing?"

"Who?"

"Miss Rippen." I start walking back and forth, doing some fancy stuff.

"No kidding." So old Brandon wouldn't mind it, either.

"What's her first name, anyway?" I ask.

"I think it's Bambi."

I miss the ball and it goes bouncing off across the grass. "You're shitting me."

"Yeah," says Brandon, and he starts laughing again. "Actually, it's Brigitte."

"Or Ginger," I say. "No, Mitzi."

"More like Titzi."

We're cracking each other up. "No, man," I tell him. "It's gotta be more dignified."

Brandon holds up his hand, like, Wait, I've got it. "Erotica."

"Erotica Rippen." We choke it out at exactly the same time, and then we're practically rolling on the ground.

We're kidding around and stuff all the way up till Chase drops me off at my place. I wave good-bye, and go upstairs to let myself in, and I'm thinking about Miss Rippen, and how my ears are still ringing from "Boot Scootin' Boogie" and "God Bless Texas," and how I really ought to scrape up the money for a basketball.

It isn't till I'm actually inside, and I'm tossing the keys on the kitchen bar, that I realize something.

I didn't dread coming home. Even though Trent closes, and he won't be here till after I've gone to bed.

I stop right where I am, between the bar and the back of the couch. It's hitting me how I've got this feeling that's so comfortable and familiar, I didn't even notice it at first.

It's that feeling of being around somebody who thinks the way I do.

CHAPTER 7

Friday, everything's back to the way I figured it'd be. I walk to school in the morning like always and head to the library to kill time till the first bell. I cut through the front foyer, just like I do every day. That's what they call the open area by the office, surrounded by glass trophy cases and backed by a glass wall that looks out over a little courtyard with a fountain and cacti and a few mangy-looking bushes. The courtyard's just for looking at. It's always locked up.

Everybody pretty much has to walk through the front foyer at one time or another—I mean, the office is right there, and the library, and the buses drop everybody off right in front of it. But the only people who hang out there before school are Brandon's crowd and their rich-guy counterparts in the other grades.

I don't care. I guess I could hang out there by myself if I wanted, but personally I'd rather be skimming the latest issue of *Sports Illustrated*.

So I'm walking through the foyer like I always do, except today I happen to glance up and see Chase. He kind of gives me that rich-guy wave, like it's only a wave if I see it. Otherwise, he could be just about to scratch his forehead or something. It's pretty stupid.

But I nod hello back anyway. I'm in a good mood because, boy, it feels good to know I'm not going to have to trudge down to that OCS room. It feels good to be *free*.

I *am* free, all day long. I get to move every time a bell rings. I get to walk out of classrooms and down halls. I get to go to my locker. Man, it's a treat, after sitting in the same old desk six hours a day.

The only time the good feeling wears thin is when the last bell rings. When I see everybody heading to their meetings, their buses, their carpools.

I'm free, all right. Free to walk home alone.

Saturday morning, I'm sound asleep when Trent wakes me up.

"Hey," he's calling from the doorway of my bedroom. "You awake?"

I mumble something into the mattress.

"Get up," Trent says, still from the doorway. "It's your birthday."

I pull the pillow over my head.

"Happy birthday to you," he starts to sing. Or bellow, actually. *"Happy birthday tooo you."*

One thing Trent cannot do is sing. It's not so bad when he's just fooling around, but when he's really belting one out at the top of his lungs, it's kind of horrifying.

"I'm awake," I say, still under the pillow.

"Happy birthday, dear Charrrleeee . . ."

He's obviously going to go into one of his big production numbers. "Shit," I groan, and then I'm sitting up. "What? What is it? It's my birthday. I want to sleep late on my birthday. Is that too much to ask?"

"Actually, no," says Trent. "But I'm about to work a double and I thought you might want your present sometime today."

I'm sitting there all bleary-eyed, and I'm thinking, Aw, shit. Because we can't afford to get me a present. And besides, I didn't get him anything for *his* birthday.

"I hope it was free," I say. Maybe they were giving away stuff at the bookstore again.

"None of your business, you old geezer. You want it or not?"

I'm sitting there, and my hair's probably sticking straight up all over my head. I'm wearing one of Trent's old Cowboys T-shirts that's been washed so many times it's gray instead of navy, and I've got on torn underwear that I'd probably be hanging out of, if I stood up. My hairy legs are sprawled out all tangled up with the sheet.

But it's my birthday, and Trent got me a present.

"Yeah, sure," I say.

"Then *catch.*" All of a sudden this basketball comes flying at me, and I get my hands up just in time to catch it. Inches away from my face.

"Shit," I say. What's he trying to do, kill me?

I lower the ball and look at it. It smells rubbery and new. It does feel kind of good in my hands. All solid. Unleaky.

It feels good. Even if I practically almost got a broken nose, even if I did get dragged out of a deep sleep at the crack of dawn, it still feels good. Somebody noticed I needed a new basketball. Somebody went to the trouble to wake me up because they remembered I was born sixteen years ago.

I give it a little toss, catch it.

Trent's standing in the doorway, arms folded, still watching me. "Thanks," I tell him. "I'll sleep with it under my pillow."

"Sure." He unfolds his arms, straightens. "Go back to sleep. See you tonight about ten-forty-five."

But after he leaves, I stay sitting up for a while, yawning and twirling the basketball around in my hands. I'm thinking how maybe I'm lucky, in a way, not to have a regular family. Because even if I didn't get a brand-new car, at least I've got my own space, and Trent won't even set foot in the doorway without my permission.

I'm thinking this, and I figure I ought to toss the ball into the corner so I can try to get some more sleep.

But the thing is, it's new. It's mine. It's a present from Trent.

I give it a spin on my fingertip. Then I kind of tuck it under my arm, and I lie down with it still tucked under my arm, and then I go back to sleep.

*　*　*

When I finally do get up, I don't eat breakfast right away. I go jogging first, and I end up taking the route down past the soccer fields. I'm thinking about birthdays and basketballs and Corvettes and file boxes locked up in closets, and for some reason, instead of threading my way through the campus like I usually do, I head down the hill through Brandon's neighborhood. Which is pretty stupid, because now I'll have to go back *up* the hill later.

The neighborhood's even nicer when you're not in a car. The air smells of trees and shaded grass, and there's a quiet that doesn't seem to have anything to do with me. It's a bought-and-paid-for kind of quiet.

For some reason I kind of like the way my feet make a slapping sound on the pavement. I can't remember which street Brandon lives on. I don't care, anyway. I don't turn on any of the streets that might be his, I just keep going to the creek, to the bike trail that leads past the playground and the basketball court.

Trent told me once that the main bike trail runs along the river, that it goes from one side of the city to the other. I figure this trail must lead to the main one somehow. And today I feel like I *could* run from one side of the city to the other.

So I head along the trail, along the soft, cracked asphalt under these huge trees past these block-long houses. And I slow my pace, so my legs won't get cranky the way they do sometimes after four or so miles. I also figure I'd better stop and get some water, because who knows where I'll end up, once I get started?

So I ease up when I come around the bend and see the playground up ahead. A lot of kids and their parents here today. Lots of cars parked on the street—so maybe this place isn't just for the rich people who live here.

I'm slowing to a walk, and I see a bunch of guys straggling off the basketball court toward the stone fountain. I know some of them, at least their names. They're all like rich-guy types. I don't see Chase, but I do see David Carlson. And Luke Cottington.

They get to the fountain before I do. I keep heading toward it anyway. I don't give a shit who's here. I'm thirsty.

They don't seem to notice me. They kind of stand there in a bunch, taking turns getting drinks, joking and messing around the way Brandon and I did yesterday.

I'm just waiting my turn. Now that I'm not moving anymore, I notice how much I'm sweating. The whole front of my tank top is dark from it.

"What's the deal with that shirt?" I hear Cottington say. I look up, but he's not talking to me. He's talking to Carlson. "You borrow that from your sister?"

Carlson's got on a yellow shirt. Not a T-shirt like the other guys. A tank top—but not big and airy like

66

mine. Tight. It does look kind of like something a girl would wear.

Still, I'm thinking how Cottington's got a bug up his butt about other people's clothes. Even his friends' clothes.

Of course, all the other guys are dressed practically alike. Kind of like Brandon was dressed yesterday. And every other day, now that I think about it.

It hits me, Brandon's crowd always does wear the same thing—jeans or shorts, and the same brand of shoes and the same style of shirt. They're like packages that have to be the same size and shape so they can fit into the same slot at the post office.

"Eat shit and die, Cottington," Carlson's saying. He ducks his head to get a drink.

"No, really, man. It's so *gay*."

I can't help it, my eyes latch right on to Cottington. I'm ready to kill him.

"All I'm saying is, it makes you look a little . . . *iffy*. That's all I'm saying," Cottington says.

It's just one of Cottington's comments, I tell myself. He's an ignorant bastard. Blow it off.

Still, I don't understand guys like Cottington. Maybe because I've grown up around Trent. I found out he was gay when I was only ten or eleven, before I even really knew what it meant—so it could be I'm just used to it. But it's not like I'm weird or anything—my friend Nick never thought it was any big deal, either.

Carlson darts his eyes around, checking out the reactions. He sees a couple of the other guys are trying not to laugh at him and his tank top. "Hey, fine," he says, a little too loud. "If it turns you on that much, I'd better take it off. To be safe." And sure enough, Carlson does it, he pulls the shirt off over his head and wads it up, small.

"It's not the *shirt* that turns me on," Cottington says, leaning over the fountain. "It's the memory of your sister, inside it." He takes a couple of slurps before he straightens, wiping his mouth with the back of his hand. Then he grins. "Or should I say *out*side it."

Everybody laughs. "Fuck you, Cottington," Carlson says, but he doesn't seem real interested. He sounds like he just wants the conversation to be over. He balls the shirt up even tighter in his hand.

Everybody starts heading back to the court. Now it's my turn to get a drink. I step forward, and I'm still keeping an eye on Cottington. I'm not going to start anything here in the middle of all his buddies. But I might not mind too much if *he* started something.

Just as Cottington's turning away, he sees me. My hand's already on the handle, the water's already spattering onto the cool rock, but I don't bend over. I just wait to see if I'm going to have the opportunity to beat the holy crap out of him.

But Cottington's not much of a mind reader. He glances on past like I'm another tree or part of the sidewalk. Then he's walking off with his buddies.

I get my drink. Nice and slow.

When I'm finished, they're all back on the court,

playing. Carlson's skinny bare chest is already heaving from the effort. His shirt is lying on the grass just far enough away from the court that you wouldn't know it belonged to one of the guys playing basketball.

I'm wondering if he'll even pick it up when they finish. Or if he'll just leave it lying there.

I never knew you had to have a dress code to play a pickup game of basketball. I can't believe Brandon brought me here yesterday in my definitely un–color-coordinated clothes and my definitely un–designer shoes.

Good for Brandon, that's what I say.

Still, I can't see inviting him over to my place again. Or should I say *our* place—mine and Trent's. Because what if he thinks the way Cottington does? It'll be a whole lot easier not to get to be friends with the guy in the first place if he's got a problem with gays.

Oh well. I gave it a shot.

I look down the trail. It winds off along the creek, into the trees.

Somehow I don't really feel like being in this neighborhood anymore. Somehow I don't even want to run *through* it.

So I start the jog back to *my* neighborhood. I head back to that long hill. I'm fresh enough to slog back up without losing too much speed.

Back up on level ground, my breath starts to match the rhythm of my legs again. Before the rhythm takes me over, I'm thinking about Nick. How Nick and I were a lot alike. How neither one of us ever cared what anybody *wore,* for God's sake. Or who some-body else screwed—except as a matter of general curi-osity.

Nick was like me. I don't do things half-assed. Either you're my friend, or you're not.

CHAPTER 8

It turns out Brandon's offering me a ride home pretty often.

And I end up taking him up on it pretty often too. Why not? It beats walking, and it's not like I'm having to do much talking or anything. And it's kind of funny watching him flip up and down the dial, trying to figure out what kind of music he does and doesn't like.

And after a month or so, I've decided old Chase is almost interesting, once you get to know him. Brandon likes books more than somebody like him should admit, and he likes trotting out ideas and running them around. And I'd never admit it, but I like to listen to that kind of stuff. And to think about it to myself, even if I'm not much of a talker. Which is okay, Brandon talks enough for two people once he gets going.

He's never asked any questions about why I wave at the kid on the red trike, but he always slows down at the junky yard. And I've noticed the last few times, when I've got the window down and all, he'll lift one hand off the steering wheel in that Leadership Committee rich-guy kind of wave. It's pretty funny, but I don't laugh.

Then one day when we're on the way home, Brandon's going on about Ayn Rand, whom I've never read, but I guess now I'll have to. We're cutting through the residential neighborhood, and I'm kind of keeping an eye out for the kid.

Up ahead I see him, he's just kind of singing or talking to himself, playing with his hands, sitting on his tricycle. His little blond head turns, and I can tell he sees us.

Then my guts kind of draw up and get heavy, because what he doesn't see is this man with an angry face charging out of the house, barreling down the sidewalk behind him.

Brandon stops talking. The man drags the kid off his trike, and I'm thinking somebody should do something because the trike's all tangled up with the kid's legs, which seems to make the guy even madder.

He jerks the kid loose. The trike falls sideways into the weeds. He's smacking the kid across the head, back, anywhere.

I shut my eyes as we get closer. I can feel Brandon slowing down, but I don't even want to see it.

Maybe the dad told the kid to come in, and he said no because I haven't waved at him yet or something. And there's nothing I can do. Because it's none of my business if some dad or stepdad wants to spank his kid.

Then my eyes have to open, because Brandon's pulling up to the curb and my window's buzzing down. He leans over, practically in my lap, yelling: "Hey, man, cut it out!"

The guy's big. I mean, like pro-football size. We're talking lineman. His eyes are round and kind of droopy along the bottom, like a bulldog's. In fact, his whole face looks somewhat like a bulldog's.

He doesn't seem to care for Brandon's input.

"Mind your own business," he snarls.

Brandon puts on his LC face. "I'm just trying to warn you," he calls, and he's using his LC voice too. "There's a cop car a block over, heading this way."

"Big fucking deal," the guy says. Then he gives the kid an extra shake, just to show that Brandon can't tell him what to do. It's kind of nauseating, like the kid's arm's about to get yanked out of the socket.

The kid cringes. But he doesn't yell. And he's not crying.

Now, I'm not a kid lover or anything. I don't like them up close, because they have a tendency to follow you around and talk at you all the time and hang on you. But the kid's arm is all tiny in that huge hairy fist, and I can see white around the rim of his eyes, he's so scared, and I'm starting to get mad at this guy.

"Stupid little *shit*," the guy says. He punctuates it with another whack across the kid's head.

I get out of the car.

"Charlie," Brandon says, and I feel him grabbing at my sleeve but I don't pay any attention. I slam the door shut, and then I'm walking toward the guy, but I don't know what I'm going to say.

The guy doesn't either. He's watching me with his

bulldog eyes, and I guess I distract him a little because the kid twists loose and scampers up the sidewalk without looking back.

Then he's inside. I stop.

The screen door bangs shut on the front porch, but the guy's bending down. He grabs this stick from the weeds by the sidewalk. It looks like an old broken broom handle.

"I don't think you ought to hit him like that," I say.

The guy takes a step toward me. The kid's inside, he's safe—I ought to go now.

But this guy's eyeing me like I'm some kind of trash that blew into his yard.

So I don't move.

"I'll do anything I goddamn please," he's telling me, and I'm looking right into those bulging eyes. "And you can fuck off."

"After you," I say.

Bad reflex.

This guy's got *good* reflexes; the broom handle comes whistling around and I barely have time to duck so it doesn't bust my head open.

I hear the squeal of tires, and the sound of an engine zooming away, and part of me knows that Brandon's booking it out of here, but most of me is lunging to get hold of the stick before the guy takes another swing.

He gets a good one in on my left arm, and then I'm hanging on, so he can't get enough room to crack me one again. My arm hurts like hell, he caught me right in the muscle, but I sure don't have time to moan about it.

Then I hear the shriek of rubber on asphalt again. And an engine roaring closer and closer.

And then a *whump!*, and the guy's like scrambling away, and I see the Corvette's jumped the curb, it's sailing right at me, across the weeds and grass.

I clutch the broom handle and shut my eyes.

Nothing happens, and when I open them, the Corvette's bumper is about two feet away from my knee and Brandon's shoving the passenger door open.

"Get in!" he's hollering.

The guy's on his porch by this time, but now that the car's stopped, he's glaring at me like he'd love to come down and finish this, but he doesn't care to get run over by Chase the Maniac.

I'm running around the car, but as I start to get in, I realize I've still got the broom handle.

"You hit that kid again," I yell, waving the broom handle at the guy on the porch, "and I'm going to come back and shove this up your ass!"

That gets him moving. He leaps over the railing, but it's too late. Brandon's got the car in gear and we're leaving tracks in the grass before I've even got the door closed.

I look back; the guy's running after us in the street, but Brandon floors it, and in about two seconds the guy's like a little ant waving his arms at us.

I'm feeling a rush of adrenaline like you wouldn't believe, and it takes me a few moments to realize Brandon's mad.

"Are you insane?" he's yelling at me. "Are you completely out of your fucking mind?"

"You're the one who stopped in the first place," I tell him, rubbing my arm. It's not broken or anything, but I bet it's going to have one hell of a bruise tomorrow.

"I was just trying to get him to *quit.* I wasn't planning on risking our *lives,* for God's sake."

We're driving along, and the adrenaline's slowly soaking back in to where it's supposed to be. And I'm starting to remember stuff. About how it used to be, with my mom.

"He's going to go inside and take it out on the kid," I tell Brandon.

"Listen to me, you asshole. We will go to the nearest pay phone. We will call the police or Child Protection or whoever we would have called anyway, if you hadn't gotten out of the fucking car!"

Brandon's pretty pissed.

I'm still holding the broom handle. I lay it down on the floorboard.

I'm thinking probably I just stirred the guy up and made him even madder.

The kid's going to be okay, I tell myself. What I'd do if I was him is, I'd run in the front door, through the house, out the back—and keep on running. Because there's not really any safe place to hide in a house with an angry parent. I learned that lesson real well—it just makes them madder, when they finally do find you.

The kid's not stupid. He took off, and he'll come

back later when things have cooled down. That's what I always did. And by the time he comes back, Brandon will have called the cops or whoever.

He's safe, I tell myself. He's all right.

I don't say any of this to Brandon. I just take a deep breath, and let it out nice and slow. Because whatever I should or shouldn't have done, the kid's not my responsibility and the whole thing's over, and everybody, even a little blond kid, gets shit on sometimes, and you've just got to learn to deal with it.

One more breath, nice and slow, to blow it off.

"Listen, thanks for coming back," I tell Brandon.

"Hey, no problem," says Brandon, real sarcastic. "Anytime you have some guy bashing your brains in with a stick, I'm available."

But his hand's trembling on the steering wheel. And now that I really look at him, he's kind of pale.

Trent's like that. Gets sarcastic when I've done something to worry him. Strange idea, that old Chase got *worried* about me.

"Look," I say, "when we get to my place, I want you to come up and sit down for a sec. Have a Coke or something. Calm down."

"*You* want *me* to calm down?"

"You don't look so hot," I tell him.

Brandon opens his mouth, then shuts it again. "What the hell did you stop and yell at him for?" he finally asks, but more quietly, like he's still pissed, but not *as* pissed.

I know this is serious, I know I could have gotten killed, but suddenly I see how I must have looked, standing there waving my arms like a madman. And the guy's bulldog face on the porch, when I told him I'd shove the broomstick up his ass. I start smiling.

"This is not funny."

I can't straighten out my mouth to save my life.

"Goddammit, it's not *funny,* Calmont."

But it is, now that we're safe.

"Maybe that's how he got bug-eyed in the first place," I say, and then I can see out of the corner of my eye that Brandon's got that trying-not-to-smile look.

I don't say anything. I'm sympathetic. It's tough to be pissed off and scared and smiling at the same time. Poor guy.

One thing you can say about old Chase, he follows through. He calls the cops and gets put on hold about a million times, but he hangs on until they actually send a guy over, and Brandon tells him what happened. Mostly. I mean, he kind of ends right before the part where I get out of the car.

When it's my turn, I'm thinking Chase could get in trouble for trying to run the bulldog guy down, so I don't bring it up either. It's not a lie if you don't bring it up and the kid's the important part, right?

The cop writes it all down, and then he leaves. And that's the last we hear of it. We figure it's better not to drive down that street anymore, not with Brandon's car like a big old silver sign saying, *Hey, bulldog man! Here's the teenagers you want to beat the living crap out of!* So we always take a right at the beginning of the block.

While we're slowing down to turn, though, we can look down and see the spot at the end of the sidewalk where the kid always waited. We can—but *I* don't. Because I don't particularly want to see this little guy on a tricycle waiting for me, when I'm never going to show.

I notice Brandon does look, but he never says anything. So probably the kid's not there anyway.

And even Brandon knows there's nothing left to do.

But he sure as hell did everything he *could* do.

Old Chase could almost grow on you, if you give him half a chance. I start to feel kind of bad, with him giving me all these rides and all, and then the thing with the bulldog guy, and Chase talking his way through all those departments to help the kid.

I figure I owe Brandon now, right? And I don't like owing people. I can't even pay him for gas, but I remember how he didn't seem to want to go home that time, so I decide it's no skin off my ass if he wants to stick around for a while instead of just dropping me off.

Turns out I was right about Chase not wanting to go home. At school he pretty much hangs with his usual crowd, but after school he starts hanging around the apartment, if he doesn't have any meetings he's got to go to.

No big deal, we just shoot baskets over at the middle school across the street, or he gets his baseball stuff out of his trunk and we hit some balls or play catch, or sometimes we just sit around by the apartment pool, and I look at the water while Brandon gets all philosophical about God and morality and the meaning of life. He ends up staying for dinner pretty often. I don't know what he tells his parents, or maybe he's just sitting down for two dinners every day.

Of course, Trent and I don't care, and I'm kind of getting used to having somebody around to break the quiet when Trent works late. And like I said, I know how it is not to want to go home.

It's funny, how someone like me and someone like Brandon Chase could have something in common.

And after a while, it gets to where Brandon's talking to Trent the way I do, instead of acting like he wants to call him "sir" all the time. And it turns out, he can keep up with Trent almost better than I can. I mean, Trent's pretty sharp, and he can zap you with words, when he wants to. But Brandon's sharp, too, when he forgets to act like he's got a ramrod up his butt.

We're eating dinner one time, and it's hot dogs and chips, and Trent's telling us how he's going to get a Ferrari when he gets rich and all.

"I'm going to get a Jeep," Brandon says. "Or a pickup, maybe. Four-wheel drive, black, with tires so big I could go off-roading through the Grand Canyon."

"A pickup," says Trent, like he doesn't believe it.

"This is your fault," he tells me. "You're a corrupting influence."

"What, 'cause he wants a pickup?"

"That's right. He was perfectly normal till he started hanging around you."

Brandon's looking at me too, like, What's Trent talking about?

"Brandon Chase," says Trent, "Boy Dynamo, Legislative Wonder, Student of the Year—until he meets . . . Captain Country."

"Aw, come on," I say.

"It's true, isn't it?" Trent turns to Brandon. "You've been listening to country music?"

"Well, some," Brandon says. "It's hard not to, when Charlie—"

"Exactly!" says Trent. "It's like when they fluoridated the drinking water. A plot to take over the U.S. of A."

Trent's in a good mood, he's having fun, and he doesn't care if we know what he's talking about or not.

"I think Charlie's right, though," Brandon says. "Once you get past the sound, the lyrics do mean more."

"Yeah?" says Trent. He's finished eating, he's going out tonight so he ate pretty fast. He gets up to take his stuff to the sink. "Like what lyrics? Name some."

When you argue with Trent, you'd better have your facts right at hand. Or don't even start.

"I heard one I liked," Brandon tells him. "But I don't know who it's by."

"How's it go?" I ask. "I might know."

"You probably do," says Trent. "And unfortunately, I probably do too. Let's hear it." He folds his arms and leans back against the counter, waiting for Brandon to present his evidence. No pressure.

Brandon picks up a potato chip, but he doesn't put it in his mouth. He's thinking. "Something about how you can lock your heart up safe." He doesn't sing, he says the words slow, and rhythmic, like the melody is pushing them into his head. "But the moment that lock clicks, you're cut off from the light." He frowns a little. "Unbreakable Heart," he announces, pointing the potato chip at Trent. "That's the name of it."

"That's Mark Crutchfield," I say.

Trent turns back to the sink and rinses off his plate. Without commenting.

"Hey," I say. "Hey, Chase, you got him. You shut Trent up. It's a first."

"Mark Crutchfield is crossover. He doesn't count," Trent says, drying off his hands.

"He sure the hell does," I say. "Admit it, Brandon's right. He shoots, he scores!"

"Shut up," says Trent, but he gives Brandon a grin as he heads to his room to change.

Brandon and I are in the kitchen cleaning up our stuff when Trent walks back through on his way out. Brandon starts humming "Unbreakable Heart." And I pick right up and join in—just loud enough to annoy Trent.

"Aw, man—shut up." He pulls the door closed behind him.

"Where's he going, anyway?" Brandon asks. I get my books and stuff, and so does he. We've got a buttload of algebra to do; there's a test tomorrow.

"Dallas. Clubbing."

"On a Tuesday?"

"He doesn't have to open tomorrow."

"Oh. Hey, you got the list of formulas? I can't find my notes."

"Right there," I tell him.

Brandon starts copying the formulas down.

"I can't believe you've got a brand-new Corvette, and you want a pickup," I tell him while I'm sifting through my folder, trying to find some papers I need.

"It's not brand-new. My dad got it used. And I never wanted it."

It may be used, but it's damn sure not more than a year old. And I don't ask him why he got it in the first place, because by now I think I know.

He tells me anyway. "My dad picked it out. He said I should get a car that would be good for dates."

"You mean, it would impress girls," I correct him. "Because a car that'd be good for dates would be like a van or an RV or something."

I'm trying to find last Wednesday's pop quiz, but I can feel Brandon looking at me. "You know," he says, like he's discovered something, "you're kind of quiet, but the truth is, you're one horny son of a bitch."

I'm flipping through my book now, I don't even

look up. "Why, yes." I say it in a professor voice, like I'm discussing physics. "Yes, I am." After all, it's only the truth.

"And the thing about it is, you don't act it, so you'll probably get laid about ten times more than I ever will."

"Why, yes, my friend," I say in my professor voice. "I probably will."

CHAPTER 9

"Where are y'all going?" asks Trent as he checks the cash in his wallet.

It's the last Saturday before Thanksgiving, and Trent's getting ready to go out tonight too. I'm waiting for Brandon.

"There's a party at this girl named Misty's house," I tell Trent.

Trent kind of eyes me.

"Well, I'm glad you're getting out," he finally says, sticking the wallet in his back pocket. "And making some friends. I was about to put an ad in the paper for you. 'Sixteen-year-old straight white male, looking for friends. Likes square dances, hog-calling contests, and country music.'"

"Beats that crap you listen to," I tell him. He's checking his hair in the mirror. "You going to Dallas?"

"No. Everybody's getting together at Matt's place. Where are my keys?"

Trent's been seeing a lot of Matt lately. I don't ask him about it, because ever since the phone threats Trent's been a little touchy about discussing his relationships. I figure it makes him feel better to keep his life divided into two compartments. It's like he thinks I'm safer that way, all neatly tucked into one side.

"On the counter," I tell him. "Under the paper."

I just don't want Trent to ask for details on where *I'm* going. I'll tell him if he asks, but I'm not sure what he'd think about going to some lake house where there's no adults around.

I'm not planning on drinking a whole lot. I just haven't been to that many parties. In fact, none. I'm kind of curious, and I figure it beats sitting around by myself, right? I think I ought to get some points for even taking one step out.

Trent doesn't ask for details. He's obviously still been weighing this party thing out in his mind, though, because as he's heading for the door, he gives me this real serious look.

"You keep your head on straight, Charlie. Don't do anything stupid."

"I won't."

"Okay," he says, stepping out onto the landing. "Have fun."

"You too," I tell him as he pulls the door shut.

It's dark on the road to the lake house, no lights, I guess because nobody wants to attract attention. Even though it's heading into late November, it hasn't gotten real cold yet, and there's still quite a few leaves on the trees.

There's a lot of cars, and as we park in among the trees and start walking up, I can see that the house isn't what I thought it'd be. I thought a lake house was like a mansion or something, but this one's small and mostly glass and shaped like an A. There's a balcony at the cross part of the A, and steps leading down to the lake.

Inside, there's people all over. I know a lot of faces and names from being around Brandon, but I don't make a point of hanging with him at school, so I don't really know anybody here.

Some people are drinking some kind of red drink out of cups, but I'm following Brandon's lead and he makes a beeline for the keg. So I end up with beer.

The first thing I notice is that parties involve a lot of wandering around. The second thing I notice is that Brandon's a barometer or something—if Brandon says I'm okay, I'm okay. I mean, people are actually talking to me, and I actually have a couple of conversations, nothing exciting, but more than I've gotten around to having before. Maybe it makes things easier that everybody's got a little alcohol in them.

Except me. When we head out onto the balcony I finally get around to taking a sip, to see if I like beer any better than I did the last time I tried it. Nope.

Practically the whole wall of the house is glass, and I can see people inside dipping the red stuff out of this punch bowl on the bar. I wonder what it is. But I don't feel like trying it with all these people around.

What if I get wasted and make an asshole out of myself?

Especially since I see Luke through the glass, coming this way. "Aw, man," I say out loud before I can help it. "Cottington's here."

"*Everybody's* here," Brandon says. He's on his second beer. No, third. I forgot he chugged the first one, to get a head start on the evening. "And Luke'll be all right. He knows you won't take anything off him."

Luke comes outside, he looks pretty relaxed, smiling and all. "Hey, where you been?" He slaps Brandon on the back, sloshing Brandon's beer everywhere. Cottington's had a few. "You two got a lot of catching up to do," he says, and he includes me when he says it.

It hits me: There's two Lukes, one for his friends and one for everybody else. And I may not be his friend, but I'm friends with his friend. I'm a friend once removed.

"Don't worry, we'll catch up," Brandon says. He gives me a grin, like, See? I told you.

Then David Carlson comes weaving across the deck timbers. When I say weaving, I mean walking kind of sideways, like John Wayne, only more so. As he gets close, I see he's got this expression on his face, like he's real surprised his feet won't quite take him the direction he wants to go.

It's kind of funny, and I start smiling.

Brandon and Luke see me smiling, and they look to see what's so funny.

"Hey, Carlson!" Brandon yells, pointing down. "The floor's that way!"

"Well, hello, Pilgrim," I say, in my best John Wayne. "It's tough when a guy's own feet keep going over to the enemy."

Brandon and Cottington start cracking jokes all over the place, and the funny thing is, I do too. It's like the three of us are buddies or something.

"Brandon!"

It's our hostess, Misty. She comes over to us and, boy, she must be bombed. She throws her arms around Chase's neck and she's like all over him.

She's short, with one of the most terrific bodies I've seen on a high-school girl. Brandon's not pushing her away, not at all. I wouldn't push her away either.

In the doorway another girl hesitates, then comes to stand between me and Luke. She doesn't say anything and holds herself so she doesn't touch anyone. Misty's friend is pretty. Her hair's dark, but I can't tell what color her eyes are. I know her face, but not her name.

"Katie," says Luke. "I thought you weren't staying."

"Me too. Hi, Charlie." I can see into her cup; she's drinking the red stuff.

"Hi," I manage to say. I'm kind of surprised anybody knows who I am.

She doesn't say hi to Brandon or Carlson, but I don't think Carlson cares, and Brandon's busy trying to take advantage of the fact that Misty's trashed. Unfortunately for Brandon, she's not *that* trashed. She kind of slides out of his grasp. But she giggles when she does it.

Brandon's not fazed. I guess he figures the night is young.

"I need another beer," Misty announces, pouting.

"Me too." Brandon's flashing that LC smile at her. "I'll get you one."

"I'll come with you," Brandon says. "Be right back," he tells me. "Maybe," he adds under his breath, so I'll know not to come looking for him in case Misty's not so picky about being groped if he can manage to get her off by herself.

"Nice ass," Luke says as Misty totters off. Which is exactly what I was thinking, but I wouldn't have said it where she could hear. Or her friend.

Misty doesn't even look around. Brandon glances over his shoulder, but he just smiles, because he recently had his hand on that nice ass.

"Have you seen Camille?" Katie asks Luke. He's got his arm around her shoulder now, but she's standing straight, not leaning against him or anything. I don't remember anybody named Camille and I could care less, so I kind of tune out while Luke explains where Camille is. He's keeping his voice down, for a change. He's almost like human, tonight. Almost.

I can smell the water in the air, I can hear it lapping down at the lakeside, like it doesn't give a damn where Camille is either. Suddenly it hits me that I'm standing here with a guy who once made fun of my shoes.

I look down at my feet. Same shoes. Maybe even in worse shape than they were a couple of months ago. So what's different?

I'm thinking I'd like to walk across the balcony, down the stairs, right down to the lake. To watch the water. To be by myself, nobody's buddy.

"You're not drinking, Charlie," Katie says.

I look down, and there's my cup, still full to the brim. It's getting to be kind of a pain, holding it, so I step back and pour the whole thing over the railing.

"Man, what a waste," Luke says as I set the empty cup down.

I'm eyeing the stairs. I'm thinking I'd better wander off anyway, because Luke's whispering something in Katie's ear.

Definitely a third wheel. I turn to head for the stairs.

"Where are you going?" Katie says, a little too fast. Her eyes are fixed on me and both her hands are clutching her cup. It hits me that maybe she doesn't want to be left alone with Luke.

"Thought I'd walk down by the lake," I tell her.

But if I ask her if she wants to come, it's like I'm butting in on Cottington's business. He acts like she belongs with him. I don't know what to do.

"Can I come too?" Katie asks.

I nod. She shrugs off Luke's arm and walks over to me. He's drunk, he must be, because I don't think he'd let anybody see him looking after her like that if he was sober. Like he'd give his right arm to have her walking toward *him*.

Now I'm remembering some stuff Brandon said at the beginning of the year about Luke going out with some girl. I'm thinking this could be a very touchy situation. So I don't even look at her. We just start walking down the stairs.

"Watch your step," I tell her, because I don't want her to trip, I don't want to have to catch her, not where Luke can see. I don't know what's going on, it could be they're dating and she's just mad at him or something.

"You've got fifth-period P.E., don't you?" Katie asks as we're heading down.

"Yeah."

"I see you out there on the field."

"No kidding." We're on the ground now. I look at her, and she's looking at me too. She really is pretty. We start walking—carefully, because it's dark out here and the ground is uneven under the trees. "What do you have fifth?"

"Creative writing."

"Must be boring, if you're looking out the window all the time."

She laughs. It's a nice laugh, kind of soft. "No, I like it. I just think better when I'm looking out the window."

"So," I say, just to keep the conversation moving, "what do you do in creative writing?"

"Right now we're critiquing short stories, and then next week we're supposed to decide on the format for the magazine." She trips a little bit, and I catch her elbow. Then I let it go. "You know, *The Quill*?"

We're at the lakeside now, so we start walking along the edge. No one's down here, and all you can hear is crickets and something deeper, like a frog or something. And the water, against the shore.

I nod. "Do you write the stuff that goes in it?" I ask her.

"Some."

I stop to pick up a rock. It's just a pebble, I toss it from hand to hand while I'm thinking.

What's it like to write something that anybody can see if they want to? Do strangers come up and say "Hey, I read your poem, and that's exactly the way I feel?"

I don't say anything, though, I just see how far I can throw the rock.

"Nobody reads it anyway," Katie says.

"I do." And Cottington doesn't, I'm sure. Cottington wouldn't go for a girl who uses words like *critiquing* and *format.* I'm relaxing a little. I scoop up a handful of rocks and start pitching them in one at a time. "What have you written?"

"Well, last year I wrote this poem about a guy sitting in a chair."

"Yeah. I remember that one."

She doesn't say anything. I glance at her, and her mouth is kind of pinched up, like I'm giving her a line and she doesn't like it.

"Was it about how he's just come back from somewhere, and he's not telling anybody anything about how he feels?" I ask, to make sure.

Her mouth is softening. "Yes."

I throw the last rock in and start walking again, with Katie beside me.

My sleeve brushes hers, I could reach down and take her hand if I wanted to. And if she'd let me.

We're crunching through all these dead leaves under a big old tree that leans all the way over us, trying to touch the water. There's no point in walking any farther because up ahead the underbrush grows right up to the lake. So I stop.

"I noticed you never said where the guy came back from." I'm standing there, looking down at her, and it hits me again how pretty she is—not flashy like Misty, but easy enough on the eyes. And for some reason I'm kind of hoping she *will* tell me where he came back from.

But she doesn't.

"Where do you think he came back from?" She sounds like she thought she'd caught me picking a lock, but now she's not sure.

I think about it. I can't remember the words, or even the title, but I remember the feeling of the guy, sitting all alone in an armchair, not talking to anybody because he's seen something too awful to talk about.

"Well," I tell her, "I got the feeling maybe he came back from a war."

Katie smiles up at me. She doesn't do that too often, I guess, because I would have noticed somebody with a smile like that.

She drains the last of whatever that red stuff was in her cup, then gives me another, even better, smile. "Is

94

it all right with you if we sit down? I only had one, but I—I don't drink too often."

I still haven't touched her, except for her elbow, though I'm kind of wanting to, by now. "Sure," I tell her.

I ought to ask about her and Cottington. But she's here and he's not, so what difference does it make? I go ahead and sit beside her, right in the middle of all these leaves. I mean, what the hell, right?

"So. What gave you the idea for it?" I ask, meaning her poem.

Katie frowns into her empty cup, like she's thinking. "It's hard to explain," she says slowly, setting the cup down. "But I think you'll understand." And with that, it's like I've broken through a wall or something. Because Katie starts talking. It's like all this stuff is spilling out of her.

She tells me about this movie she saw, and her uncle who came back from Vietnam and the government classified him one hundred percent disabled because his mind was all screwed up. And how he killed himself before she was born.

She's telling me all this, very softly, and I just listen. When she finishes, I nod, because I don't really have anything to say, and then I'm looking out over the lake. There's this light breeze; it feels good on my face, and the water's real pretty at night. If I look hard, I can see all the different colors—silver and white breaking and rolling the blackness into waves.

"What are you thinking about?" Katie says.

I shrug. "Wind feels good."

I shouldn't look at her, but I do. She's all busy feeling the breeze too—she's really thrown herself into it, like she doesn't want to miss even a molecule of air. She's got her eyes shut, her head tilted back. Her hair is spilling back from her face, her neck spills down into the unbuttoned collar of her shirt.

"I was thinking if I could paint." I tell her all of a sudden, and it kind of surprises me that I told the truth like that. But it shouldn't matter; she's probably half drunk anyway. Isn't she? I mean, she said she doesn't drink often, and she's been telling me all this really personal stuff, more than I wanted to know even. And look at the way she's feeling the breeze. Nobody who was sober would do that.

"You mean like paintings? Like an artist?"

"Yeah."

She clasps her hands around her knees, and she's got her eyes open now, looking at me. "What would you paint?"

"The water."

"You mean the lake?" Her cup's half rolling, half blowing away, but she doesn't notice. She's looking out at the lake, trying to see what I saw in the water. She's very intense, Katie is. Open or shut. All or nothing.

A leaf flutters down and sticks in her hair. She's all wrapped up in seeing the lake, so I kind of take the leaf out for her. Her hair's soft under my fingers.

"The moonlight's like a road, isn't it?" she says, almost to herself. "It divides the water the way a highway divides the grass."

And I guess she's right. It does. "But do you see all the colors?" I ask her. "It's not just black. It's all different shades of black." I should feel really stupid, saying something like that. But I don't.

"Like pieces of shadows," she says. "And sparkles."

"On top of the shadows," I add.

She's just staring out at the water and then she says, *"Yeah."*

The way she says it, kind of low and breathy and amazed, tenses up my insides. Like somebody's in there, tuning up a violin. And I know what they're getting ready to play.

So when she stops looking at the water and looks at me again, I kind of lean over and kiss her.

Not too long. I'm getting kind of horny, but the horniness has the tiniest bit of something else dragging it down.

It's the way she took my thoughts and put them into words better than I could.

Now, I wouldn't mind fooling around for a while. In fact, if she wasn't so goddamn *serious* I wouldn't mind nailing her, but I don't want to get tangled up in anything. So I pull back.

But not very far. Because Katie's not ready for me to pull back, I can tell. Her lips are soft, and they've barely started to open, and she's like a magnet or something—I have to kiss her again.

I'm hardly even touching her, I don't want to get too involved here, but she slides her arms around me. And it's not like I can just sit there and not respond. I mean, I'm not a rock, am I?

She smells good, like—what? Like wildflowers, and soap, and drawers full of lacy things, and after a while it's like her lips aren't enough; I've got to taste more—her face, her hair, her neck, and one of my hands slips around to the front of her shirt. My hand's fed up with the way I'm taking this too slow.

She doesn't pull back. The fabric's covering all kinds of softness, and after a while my fingers get restless, and they start seeking out buttons. I don't stop them, she doesn't stop them, and pretty soon they're finding their way over her skin.

I'm thinking she'll push my hand away. Instead, she presses against me and pretty soon both my hands don't give a good goddamn if I get caught up or not, they're on a search mission from headquarters, and at some point I hear her give this little gasp, and after that gasp there's only one thing, one thing, and every button and zipper and snap is in the way.

I kind of ease her back onto the ground, and she doesn't seem to know what to do, but her arms stay around me and all, and they'd better, because I'm not sure I could stop if I wanted to.

CHAPTER 10

"So, did you do her?" Brandon asks after I finally find him waiting by the front door. I figure the booze must be about gone because the party seems to have lost its focus.

"Yeah," I say. We start walking toward the car. There's not near as many cars as there were.

"Shit. It figures. I came away with nothing. *Nothing!*"

I shrug. How long have I been gone?

"And I wouldn't tell Cottington if I were you. He's been trying since school started."

"Don't worry," I tell him.

"So, how was it?"

"Fine," I say. To tell the truth, I don't want to talk about it. I mean, it was great and all, but I feel like I'm doing something wrong when it's over and I'm pulling up my pants and she's trying to get everything back on and it's kind of embarrassing. It's like there's something I'm supposed to say, but I don't know what it is. I guess in old movies you lie there and smoke a cigarette or something. But this isn't the movies.

The whole thing reminds me of the only other girl I ever did it with, Megan Dunlop. That was over the summer, and I lost count how many times we did it. They were all fine, more than fine, in fact they were all fantastic, but this one time she cries when we're finished and says how she loves me. Then she asks how I feel about her.

The thing is, there's nothing to say. I *don't* feel anything about her. I mean, she's nice and all, and I appreciate her, but I know I don't love her. And she's sitting there expecting me to say something, and I can't even tell her I like her. Because I'm not sure I do. And I can't say "I don't *dis*like you," because that would be pretty rude after I just, you know.

She called me a few times after that, but I never called her back. I should have, I know. I should have lied, too, and told her whatever she wanted to hear. But I couldn't.

Maybe that's what Katie wanted to hear—that I loved her. Maybe that's what you're supposed to say when you're finished. Maybe that's what keeps it from being embarrassing. But I just can't do it.

"Fine? Is that all?"

"What do you want, a report?" I say. "Maybe I should've had her fill out a comment card."

Brandon starts laughing. " 'The service I received was—A, excellent.' "

I can't help it. I smile.

" 'And the temperature,' " Brandon continues, " 'was—A, hot. They could have heard me moaning in China.' "

It feels good to put a little distance between me and the evening. It feels good to be putting distance between me and the lake house. We're coming up to Brandon's car, shining dull silver in the moonlight.

"So, did she?" Brandon asks, digging in his pocket for his keys.

"Did she what?"

"Moan."

"Shit, I don't know." Although I do.

"My guess is yes. She looks like a moaner." He pulls out the keys, and stops in front of the car. "Listen, do you mind driving?"

I trip over a tree root, but catch myself on the hood.

"Or did you get around to actually drinking?"

"No," I say. "Beer's not my beverage of choice."

"They had that other stuff."

"What was it, anyway?"

"From what I understand, it was a little bit of everything."

It's what Katie was drinking.

"That's what I admire about you, Charlie," he says, tossing the keys to me. "You come to a place where the entire point of the evening is to drink, and you drink . . . nothing."

"Hey," I point out. "I'm going home happy."

"No shit," Brandon says. "Well, I am too, 'cause I got drunk even if I didn't get lucky. That's why I need you to drive, old buddy. I can still beat curfew, if we go now."

"Won't your folks know you've been drinking?"

"No." He walks around to the passenger side. "I can walk straight, and they won't get close enough to smell it."

I'm looking at the keys. The one to the Corvette has a black plastic cap on it. "I don't have a license," I remind him.

"I can't keep my eyes focused yet. You can drive all right, you've practiced."

And it's true, I have. In the parking lot.

"You've got a choice, Charlie. Either you drive without a license and we go home and sleep it off, or I drive with a buzz and we end up smashed into a tree. Then we'll really be up shit creek."

"All right," I say, unlocking the driver's side door. But only because I think I can handle it.

The shifting's a little rough at first. And I guess I'm probably driving too slow, since everybody's passing me.

But I pay close attention, and the shifting gets better fast, and it doesn't take long till I'm zipping along like everybody else.

I feel like I'm flowing right over the ground, like there's no wheels under the car, just air, like I'm part of the car and it's part of me, and Brandon's part of the car too.

I'm thinking if you put Brandon and me together you'd have one hell of a guy, because he'd be able to get drunk, screw around like a son of a bitch, then drive himself home sober in a goddamn sports car, without thinking how maybe he should have at least made sure Katie had a ride home.

Now Cottington, I bet he could have walked away without even offering her a hand up off the ground. Cottington's not too bright, but I bet he never felt bad about anything in his life.

Not that I feel bad. Some things just take a little longer to blow off. Like not knowing why you can't look somebody in the eyes after you've just finished fucking them.

But it's over and done with, and my body is very relaxed and pleased with the evening's events, and I know it won't be long at all before the rest of me is relaxed too.

This evening has a moral for me *and* for Brandon: If you know who to trust, you won't get hurt. You won't get dragged down. You won't get in a wreck. It's like math, if you know when to cancel out, you'll always get the right answer.

It isn't until I get to the turnoff for Brandon's neighborhood that it hits me.

"Shit," I say. I can't think and drive at the same time, so I kind of gingerly pull over to a service station.

"What? What?" Brandon's saying. "What's the matter?"

"If I drive to your house, I'll have to walk home. If I drive to *my* house, you're going to have to drive yourself home."

"Oh." He's trying to think. "Well, I guess I can make it. It's only a couple of miles. I've done it before. I just slap myself when I start phasing out—"

"Hey," I say. "Why don't you just spend the night on our couch? Call your parents and tell them something."

Brandon nods. "Yeah. All right."

So I drive to our apartment. I'm pretty proud, pulling in a parking space. No tickets, no accidents. Nobody even flipped me off, so I must have done okay.

Trent's home, and he's still up. He's watching some old movie, which means he's been waiting for me. I figure I won't bring up the driving thing.

"Okay if Brandon sleeps on the couch?" I ask as we're walking in the door.

"Sure," says Trent. "How was the party?"

"Fine," I say.

"It was excellent," Brandon announces. Most people probably couldn't even tell Brandon's had too much to drink, he's not sick or sleepy or acting stupid. The only thing that gives him away is, maybe he's walking a little too straight, and maybe he's talking a little too loud.

"He's got to call home," I tell Trent.

Brandon knows where the phone is; he picks it up and dials. Of course Trent and I aren't looking or anything.

"Hey, Mom." He's using his LC voice. "This is Brandon. Listen, we're at Charlie's apartment. . . . Me and Charlie. . . . No, we left the party a while back. Some people were starting to drink, and we decided we'd better leave. . . . Yeah. . . . Listen, we're having trouble getting the car started. . . . No, don't wake Dad. It's just the battery. I left the lights on. . . . Yeah, but he's already asleep. I can wake him up, if you want, but Charlie was saying why don't I just sleep here, and let him give me a jump in the morning. . . . Uh-huh. I know. I'll be back by then. . . . I will. Thanks. See you."

Click.

"So," Trent says as Brandon comes around to sit on the couch. I'm in the armchair. "Tell me about this party."

Brandon doesn't say anything. He's waiting to follow my lead.

"Brandon had more fun than I did," I say. Brandon gives me this look that means *yeah, right.*

"I can tell Brandon had more fun than you did," says Trent. "How the hell did you get home?"

That's Trent for you. Cuts right to the chase. "I've been meaning to talk to you about something," I say. "I think I might need to get a driver's license."

Trent doesn't say anything for a minute. "Don't tell me *you* drove."

"It was me or him," I say. Brandon's just sitting there, kind of still. Probably wondering in his fuzzy little brain if Trent's going to yell at us. Though he should know better by now.

"Do you know what'll happen if you get caught? They might take you and put you in a foster home."

I hadn't thought of that.

"And I don't like being lied about on the phone. Hear me, Brandon?"

"Yeah," Brandon says. "Sorry."

"Next time call me and I'll come get you."

"Okay," says Brandon.

"Charlie? You hear me?"

"I don't think I'll be going again anyway," I tell him.

"Why not?" Trent asks, not because he's arguing, but because he's curious.

"Because I'm not all that big on drinking, and all there is to do out there is drink," I say.

Brandon splutters, then he's cracking up all over the place.

"*Mostly* all there is to do," I say. Brandon's laughing his head off. "Will you shut up?" I tell him. Because Trent might think we're keeping something from him.

"What else is there to do?" Trent asks us, dead serious, and I know he's thinking about drugs.

I don't say anything.

"Get laid," says Brandon, and he's practically rolling on the floor.

"Will you shut up?"

But Trent's looking at me now. Pretty sharp, Trent is. "Did you use anything?" he asks.

It takes me a minute to figure out what he means.

"I didn't have anything with me," I say.

"You didn't have anything with you." Trent hasn't moved, his legs are still stretched out on the coffee table, and you'd think he was completely relaxed, but I can tell I just made him mad. "So why did you do it?"

"I kind of got caught up in the moment," I tell him.

"Is your brain located in your dick or something?"

"Next time I'll—"

"*Next* time?" Trent sits up. "It only takes one time."

"Shit, I'm sorry," I say.

"Sorry's not going to help if she's pregnant. If you've caught some disease."

"I didn't catch a disease," I tell him, kind of annoyed. I don't like being nagged, and I just happened to make a mistake. "It was her first time, all right?"

Brandon was settling down, but that sets him off again. "Cottington's going to shit," he says to no one in particular.

"It's none of Cottington's business," I point out.

But Trent's not finished. "What are you doing sleeping with someone you met at a party? Do you even know her?"

I don't say anything.

"Do you even know her name?"

"Katie," I say.

"Katie what?"

I don't say anything.

"Garrett," says Brandon, all helpful. "She's all right, Trent. She's about as straight as they get."

I'm pretty pissed by now, at Trent. Because what he's saying makes me feel like somebody he can't trust to do the smart thing. Like some kind of moron who can't control his urges. Like a kid who *needs* to be talked to this way.

Like a guy who'd pop a girl's cherry, then walk off without saying hardly anything, leaving her standing by herself in a pile of dead leaves.

"Charlie—" Trent starts, but then he kind of sighs. "All right . . . all right. There's no point in getting worked up about it now, I guess. But—"

"From now on I'll have one with me," I tell him, and I mean it. Anything to avoid this scene again. "And if I don't, I won't let it get that far."

"Assuming you don't get caught up in the *moment,*" Trent says, all sarcastic.

Brandon tries to lighten things up. "Maybe you need a warning label or something," he tells me. " 'Do not operate this machinery without proper equipment.' "

"Maybe you should get it tattooed on," Trent adds, and Brandon winces. "Down where you can't miss it. That'll remind you."

"They don't make tattoos that big," I say, which cracks Brandon up again. "Maybe if we hire a billboard painter."

"With a microscope," Trent says. He's halfway smiling when he says it, but only halfway.

CHAPTER 11

We lounge around watching the movie with Trent. It's *The Dirty Dozen,* which is perfect for forgetting anything or anybody you might not be wanting to think about.

It's been long enough that Brandon's getting sobered up. The thing is, as he's sobering up, he's getting awfully quiet, for Chase. It's like at the park that time, and maybe a couple of times since. The party button's off, the Leadership Committee button's off—which usually leaves just Brandon. But this Brandon is just sitting there on the couch, he doesn't seem to be really watching the movie. I'm thinking that maybe as the alcohol leaves, his unhappy side is filling up the vacuum.

"I wish I never had to go home," he says out of the blue, during a commercial.

Looks like I was right. I don't know what to say, so I get up and get me a Coke. I got thirsty watching everybody drink all that beer.

"Y'all want some popcorn?" I ask from the kitchen.

"Sure," says Trent. So I start nuking up a bag in the

microwave, then hop up on the counter to wait. I can watch TV over the bar if I want to.

Brandon's sitting there on the couch, and I can only see the back of his head, but somehow I know he's working himself into one of his bad moods. It makes me kind of uncomfortable, I don't know why. I mean, it's no skin off my ass if he's in a bad mood.

Still . . .

"Seems like parents expect more out of their kids than they do from themselves," I say, because that's how you get out of bad moods, you either get physical till your body's tired, or you talk until your brain's tired. So I'll get Brandon talking.

"Mine expect the fucking world out of me," says Brandon, but he doesn't look around. It's like he's talking to himself, not to me or Trent.

The popcorn's going good now. I can smell it.

"Everything I do is wrong," Brandon's saying. "Every single thing. And when I do something right, they don't even notice. They only notice what I do wrong."

"That's kind of weird," I say. The microwave beeps at me, but I don't move yet. Sometimes there's a few kernels that still need to pop. "Since you're in every advanced class there is, and on the Leadership Committee, and all that other shit you do. You're like the poster boy for student achievement."

"You know what my dad said when I got elected to LC? He said, 'Why didn't you go for treasurer? You're good with numbers.' "

"Well, that's kind of a compliment. Sort of," I say. I slide off the counter and get a big bowl.

"Why don't you tell him how you feel?" Trent says. It's the first comment he's made. "He probably doesn't even know how he sounds."

The movie's back on, but Brandon doesn't seem to notice. "He doesn't give a shit how I feel. Neither of them do. I could die tonight, and they'd just be pissed 'cause the undertaker didn't comb my hair right or something."

I'm burning my finger on the steam coming from the bag, because I don't feel like getting a pot holder. "Shit," I say.

"Just last year," Brandon's saying, "my dad wouldn't speak to me for three days because I dropped a pop-up in baseball. I was catcher, you know. Last year."

I didn't know. Neither did Trent, but he doesn't say anything either. He just listens, waiting for Brandon to go on.

I'm waiting for the bag to cool.

"Dad stomps around the house like he really wishes he was stomping *me*. And Mom just disappears like she always does when Dad's in a mood. You know, into Junior League and that sorority charity crap she does. Neither one of them ever thought that maybe I already felt bad about it," Brandon goes on, and his voice is tight with anger. "I mean, right when it happened, I felt it fall out of my glove, and I knew right then I'd blown it. I didn't need three days of them heaping it on."

Trent's shaking his head slowly, like, Tough deal.

"Sometimes," Brandon says, "I think the only thing that would make either one of them give a flying fuck how I feel is if I took one of my dad's guns and blew my brains out right in front of them."

I'm thinking, *bad* is the wrong word for the kind of mood he's talking about. Maybe Brandon's moods can slip beyond bad, into *dark*.

"It'd be great, because no undertaker could fix it up, and my dad would be stuck with this crappy-looking corpse for all his business associates to see."

I'm thinking, I should have kept my mouth shut and let him be in whatever mood he wanted to be in. It takes me a moment to remember I'm supposed to be pouring the popcorn into the bowl.

"But the thing is," Brandon goes on, all intent, like he's really planning this out. "The mess would give my mom an excuse to redecorate, and then my dad would get off telling the carpet layers and the painters what a shitty job they were doing. They'd end up loving it. I don't know," he sighs. "Maybe sleeping pills are the way to go."

I don't bring the popcorn around, because it seems funny. *Let's have some popcorn and discuss suicide.* Yeah, right.

"I was suicidal a lot when I was your age," Trent says. Brandon doesn't say anything, so Trent goes on. "I think it made it worse that I felt unconnected to people. Because nobody I knew had been there. It was like being in Mordor, like in *The Lord of the Rings*. A Mordor of the mind."

Brandon's still not saying anything, but he's watching Trent very closely, like every word has to be caught up as it comes out of Trent's mouth. I'm just listening. I know this about Trent, but it still makes me uncomfortable to hear it said out loud.

"Now I think maybe I was trying to figure out who I was, and who I wasn't, and at the same time I was being boxed in by . . . well, I guess Charlie's told you about our parents. Dad left when Charlie was born, and Mom was too drunk to remember her own name most of the time, much less that she had two kids. She died when I was still in high school."

Trent doesn't sound uncomfortable at all. "I think," he goes on, all conversational, "maybe a lot of teenagers go through that pain of trying to figure out where they fit in, what kind of personality they want to have. But most of them have a home, where they can be safe when they're ready for a break from figuring it out. I didn't. And I think maybe you don't."

Brandon kind of gives this little snort, like, You got that right.

"Maybe when you're tired of being Brandon Chase, Big Man On Campus or Brandon Chase, Party Animal, you go home, and all you hear is somebody telling you how much you miss the mark. My guess is they don't mean it that way. My guess is they don't know how they sound. It doesn't matter anyway, because you can't make them change. You can only try to survive, and make sure *you* don't turn out like that. It's just too bad your home's not a safe place for you. I

113

know how that is. It sucks, because you don't get any breaks."

I'm thinking how nobody would figure on this from Brandon. He's got such an upbeat, open kind of image. I'd bet he's never told anybody what he just told Trent.

Brandon finally looks away. He clears his throat. Trent turns back to the movie, so I bring the popcorn around and plunk myself down on the couch. The movie's almost over; they're to the part where Charles Bronson and Lee Marvin are leaving the castle. Nobody says anything, and nobody's eating any popcorn. Except me. I start crunching away, because I am not going to let this conversation drag me down.

"I envy you," Brandon says, and I realize he's talking to me. "You could live through a massacre and sprawl out like it's algebra class or something. Nothing ever gets to you. You don't care about anything."

That kind of pisses me off. "How do you know what I care about?" I ask him. "Are you a mind reader?"

"Take it easy," Brandon says. "All I'm saying is you don't worry about stuff. I mean, like you don't care if people see you not drinking, and you don't care about letting anybody know you got laid. That kind of stuff."

"Why should I care about any of that?"

"That's what I'm saying. Most people do."

"He's giving you a compliment, Charlie," says Trent. He reaches over and takes a handful of popcorn. "Charlie cares," he tells Brandon. "He just chooses what he's going to care about."

"Yeah," I say. "I'm picky."

"All right. Name one thing," says Brandon, and I swear to God he sounds like Trent. "Just one thing you ever cared about."

"Hey, if you want to care about stuff," I tell him, "go ahead. If you don't want to, don't."

Brandon looks at Trent.

Trent shrugs. "Might as well try to get him to discuss particle physics," he tells Brandon. He grabs the bowl out of my hand and offers it to Brandon. They both start munching.

For some reason his words sting. I don't know why, but they do. Maybe because it's partly Trent's fault I don't talk about things. And partly my mother's. And partly mine.

Mostly mine, I guess.

Suddenly I remember something I haven't thought about in years. It happened when I was maybe eight or so, and I never even told Trent. What happened was my mom was having one of her bad days, and she told me to go to the store to get her a bottle of wine. I didn't want to, but she was having one of those days where you better not cross her. So she gives me money, and writes a note to the clerk and everything, about how I have permission to pick it up for her.

Of course, I was just a kid, so the clerk wads it up and tosses it and tells me to get out of there. He tells me if he ever sees me again he'll call the cops.

I was scared to go home after that, so I went and hung around the loading dock of the grocery store till Trent got off work. I must have been there three or four hours, and that's what I remember most about the whole thing, sitting there on the hard concrete, hoping a truck didn't come so I wouldn't have to move, and hoping my mom went and got the wine herself so she'd at least be passed out when Trent and I got home.

And that's what happened; we got home and she was on the middle of the living room floor. She'd pissed her pants, and Trent got her cleaned up and put to bed. I didn't help him, and I never told him what she'd done because he'd get mad, and when she woke up they'd get in one of those huge old fights. And after she died, I never got around to telling him because, why make him think about it? So he never even knew I'd been sitting out there all those hours.

The thing is, I don't know why this seems like something I ought to be telling all of a sudden. It's no big deal, and it was a long time ago. And it doesn't have anything to do with proving I care about stuff.

"I wish I could be more like you, man," Brandon's saying. "I mean, if you care too much about things, it just drags you down."

"But if you don't let yourself care at all," Trent says, "it's like you're living in a box."

"Uh-oh," I tell Brandon. "Trent's getting philosophical. Watch out."

But Brandon sits up like somebody jolted him with an electric current. "No, he's right." It's a kick, the

116

way Brandon can get all excited over some idea. "Caring about things opens you up to be hurt." He sounds like he's discovered the formula for gold or something. "But if you don't do it, if you don't open yourself up, it's like you've shut yourself up in a box."

The credits start rolling. "The end of this is all wrong," Trent says. "Everybody's killed off. More of them should have made it."

I sit up. "If only they had cared more," I tell Brandon, all fake-excited, "if only they had opened themselves up, they wouldn't be going out in a box."

Brandon throws a handful of popcorn at me. In about two seconds the place is like a blizzard, and Trent's ducking for cover. Then we use the cushions off the couch, and it's kind of wild for a while.

By the time we slack off, all the popcorn is tromped into the carpet, but we have to clean it up tonight because if we don't the roaches will take over. I mean, like pull up a moving van and unload, while we're asleep.

"I knew all that LC experience would come in useful someday," I tell Brandon. "You know just how to pick up trash."

"*You* ought to join something," he says. "At least go to dances or something. We could double."

"You ought to, Charlie," Trent agrees, coming back in from the kitchen. He doesn't help, he just plops down on a chair. "It'd be good for you."

It's like they're ganging up on me or something.

"Oh, yeah," I say, and I say it kind of sarcastic so they'll lay off.

But when everything's cleaned up, when I'm lying in bed, when Brandon's asleep on the couch and Trent's snoring in his room, I can practically feel the hard concrete slab of the loading dock under my ass, and the way the tears burned when I squeezed my eyes shut to make them go back inside.

It takes me a while to blow it off, but when I finally do relax, my eyes shut gentle, with no burning.

The only thing is, now I see sparkles and shadows rippling across the back of my lids. And I can just almost hear a girl's voice, low and serious.

So I roll over and put my pillow over my head, before I start smelling lacy things, or feeling a dark softness that's not really there.

CHAPTER 12

The first time Brandon ever mentioned I could meet him in the front foyer before school, I blew him off. And the second time. And then he blew it off too. It's not like I'm the only friend he's got. He's still Mr. Popularity, and he's still pretty heavy into the Leadership Committee and all that.

But a week or so after the party, I get to school a little early. The halls are kind of empty, and I'm figuring, what the hell, I'll go check out the front foyer. It won't kill me to make a little effort—the party turned out okay, didn't it?

I walk past the library, and I can see the front foyer through the glass windows. Brandon's not there yet. Hardly anybody's there. Just these loose, half-formed bunches of people.

"Hey, Calmont," someone says, and then I see him, Luke Cottington, standing in the middle of what's starting to form into Brandon's crowd.

I haven't seen him since the party. I'm thinking maybe he has something to say about how I went off with his girlfriend, or whatever he thinks she is.

But he doesn't look pissed. Maybe he was too drunk to remember. Or maybe he never really cared.

So I head on over. I hear a couple of hi's—so I do it, I actually say hi back. One general, all-purpose "hi," for everybody.

"You seen Chase?" Cottington asks.

Misty-with-the-great-bod is here, she steps aside so I can stand beside her. It hits me that the rich-guy circle is forming right now, with me in it.

"No," I say. I've got a book under my arm, and I shift it to the other side, and I notice Misty's watching me.

Okay, maybe there's some polite thing I'm supposed to say. Since I kind of met her at the party and all.

I don't have a clue what it is, though. So I just kind of nod hello at her. That must be okay, she smiles back—quick, like she was waiting for me to go first.

Which is not the impression I had of her at the party, let me tell you.

"He's got my fucking calculator," Luke's complaining. "He's had it since Friday."

I shrug.

"He'll be here," some guy tells him. "Chill."

"You chill." Luke's scanning the front foyer. "I've got a test. The fucker better not be late," he adds.

"Here's the fucker now," somebody says, and sure enough, Brandon's nudging his way in beside me. He doesn't say hello or anything, he's just pulling Luke's calculator out of his backpack, but he gives me a quick grin to let me know he's going to share this

120

Kodak moment with Trent later. "Don't tell me," he says to Luke, "you've been having a cow."

"More like a fucking elephant." Luke closes his hand around the calculator like Brandon's just passed him the Holy Grail.

"Don't you know any other adjectives?" Misty bursts out. "There's a whole dictionary full of them."

"Yeah," Luke says. "But *fuck*'ll cover anything." He seems more relaxed, now that the calculator crisis is over. "More *bang* for the buck."

Some of the guys laugh. I can't help it, I kind of smile, but then I notice Misty's watching me again. The second she sees me looking at her, her eyes dart away.

"I've got to go to my locker," Brandon says to me. "You need to go to yours?"

I shrug. We're not supposed to go to our lockers before the bell rings, but I figure nobody'll come down on Brandon the LC man. And the bell will be ringing pretty soon anyway.

Brandon slings his backpack over his shoulder and turns away. As I start to follow him I see Katie slip into the circle across from me.

It's just for a split second—and in that split second, I think maybe she sees me too—but I don't know for sure, because I don't stop. I don't even slow down.

I just catch up with Brandon.

So Brandon and I are walking down the hall, and he's like on the campaign trail, as usual. The funny thing is, some of the people are saying hi to me too.

I don't say anything. I already said hi once this morning. I'd feel stupid, saying it over and over again the way Brandon does.

So I just nod.

"You see the way Misty was looking at you?" Brandon asks.

I shrug.

"You think maybe Katie told her something?"

It happened. It's over. What's there to tell?

"Like what?" I ask.

"Like how you measured up," Brandon says. "Maybe girls, like, rate guys or something."

"She seemed to like it okay."

"*Seemed* to. But how do you know?"

"Shit, Chase. I was *there*," I tell him.

"I know you were *there*. I'm just saying, how do you know she wasn't just being polite?"

"Polite's got nothing to do with it. You can tell. Like maybe not with a hundred percent accuracy, but I'd say ninety-eight, ninety-nine percent." It's kind of funny, and I smile.

"Man, I wouldn't be laughing. I'd be worried she'd be comparing me to everybody else."

"She doesn't have anybody to compare me *to*," I point out as the bell rings. "And she's not like that anyway."

Brandon gives me kind of a funny look when I say that. He doesn't say anything, though, he just stops at his locker and I keep walking the ten feet down to my locker.

I'm twirling the combination dial. "You ought to ask her out," he calls. "It's practically a sure thing."

Then he realizes where he is and looks around real quick. Because he's talking about Katie, and Cottington's locker is right next to Brandon's. Chase isn't trying to make trouble, he's just trying to get me laid.

I'm looking for my algebra book. I don't mention Brandon's the one who needs help getting laid, not me.

He lowers his voice. "It wasn't even a date." Brandon tosses his backpack on the bottom, instead of hanging it up. His locker is starting not to be as tidy as it was at the beginning of the year.

Still, it only takes him about five seconds to find his algebra stuff. He slams the door shut and comes over. "One of us should be getting some," he says.

"No," I tell him, digging through the stuff at the bottom of my locker. "She'd be expecting all this shit."

Brandon leans against the locker next to mine. I can feel him looking at me. "Too intense, too fast," I hear him say, like he's added something up.

I shrug. I'm actually not too surprised that he knew what I was talking about. Like I said, old Chase is pretty sharp.

And I'm not even sure Katie *would* go out with me. I mean, I left her there and all. And I didn't call. Though it did cross my mind a couple of times.

I finally find my algebra book.

"Uh, hi," I hear Brandon say to somebody as I'm standing up.

"Hi."

I kind of glance up, and the world gets very still and quiet all of a sudden. Because it's Katie.

Brandon's standing there behind her, and he grimaces, like, *I swear I didn't know she was around.*

"Can I talk to you?" she asks me.

"Yeah. Sure," I say to her, and the world starts getting noisy again, locker doors slam, people move down the hall, talking. Brandon gives me a look that repeats his entire argument about asking her out, and then he's gone.

I'm standing there, but I don't shut my locker. It's like if I shut my locker, this is serious or something. I'm wondering what she wants to talk to me about. I hope it's not a Megan Dunlop kind of thing. Although that's pretty conceited, to think that.

"So. How's it going?" I ask her, while I'm pretending to look for a notebook.

"Listen," she says, "I'm not good at leading up to things, or playing games. I was wondering if . . . Did I do something wrong?"

Her voice kind of shakes at the end. I'm thinking maybe she figures she's some kind of sexual klutz. And she's not.

"No," I say. I've got my hand on the shelf, and I'm trying not to look at her.

But she doesn't say anything, so I kind of have to make sure she's okay, the way I didn't after helping her to her feet that night. I don't look at her face, though.

She must have a lot of homework; she's loaded down with books. She's got a spiral notebook pressing into the skin of her arm, and you can tell it's going to leave marks.

"You didn't do anything wrong," I tell her books. She still doesn't say anything.

"You were great," I tell the top button of her shirt. "It's just me, all right? It's just, I'm not . . ."

I kind of accidentally look into her eyes, and I can't think what it is that I'm not. They're bluish gray, with long lashes, and so serious you could just about be hypnotized if you look at them too long.

I look back into the locker, but I can't remember if I've got everything I need.

"Charlie," she says, and her voice is still shaking. "I was hoping maybe we could be friends. Just friends, like talk and stuff, sometimes."

After she says it she just stands there, perfectly still, waiting, so I have to look at her again. This time I notice there's one lock of perfect shining hair that's hanging forward over her shoulder; my hand kind of wants to brush it back with the others. But I don't move.

It's like I'm on the edge of something, and I can't tell if it's pleasure or pain, and the thing is, there's no way to know until I'm already in over my head. All I know is, it's trying to suck me down, and I'm not like Brandon or Luke or a million other people, I don't have a clue how to just go out and care for somebody.

I wouldn't even know how to start. I'm different from all the humans who seem to be born knowing, born with the instinct all developed. In this one area I'm like an unformed animal, blind and weak and stupid. And nobody knows it. Nobody sees.

But you can bet Katie would see it.

She's standing there with all those heavy books. Waiting.

Friends, my ass.

There's nothing I need out of my locker. I shut the door. "I can't," I tell her. "Thanks, though." I turn away.

Luke Cottington's at his locker now, down by Brandon's. He just kind of catches my eye—or maybe Katie's. And then he looks away, back into the open locker.

I start walking. I figure he didn't hear anything. Or probably he just doesn't care. I mean, Cottington was busting a gut over a *calculator,* for God's sake.

I pass him, and he doesn't even seem to notice. He's just frowning into the shelves like he can't figure out what *he* needs, either.

Brandon's already in algebra when I get there. He's just sitting on his desktop, talking to a couple of people and laughing, and I'm actually relieved to see him. I don't have two compartments, like Trent. I've only got one, and you're either in or you're out. Trent's in. Brandon's in.

Katie's out.

I slide into the desk behind Brandon, and we're

joking around, and it's great to have a friend like this, where you don't have to put things into words, you just know how it is. Where a deep conversation means listening to Brandon talk about stuff that doesn't have anything to do with shit like feelings.

CHAPTER 13

We haven't gone to Brandon's house since that one time, and I've never seen his parents. Which is fine with me. I'd rather not meet anybody's parents.

But then, not long after Brandon spends the night, the Chases invite me to their house for dinner.

Brandon doesn't say much about it when he delivers the message, in fact I get the impression he'd rather I didn't come, but I still say okay. It's my policy never to pass up a free meal. And, I figure if his parents are as tight-assed as he says, they're wanting to make sure I'm not a bad influence or anything. Though I'd say I'm probably the opposite, since I don't keep a booze supply hidden in my closet.

So one day I go to Brandon's house instead of to my place, and we kind of hang around, with Brandon showing me how to play all these video games until his parents get home.

Mrs. Chase gets home first. She comes to the door of the living room we're in, and she's got that rich-lady look, blond hair and very tan and slim.

Brandon's like a mummy or something, he doesn't really look at her, and just mumbles answers, though as far as I can tell she's just asking regular mom stuff like how was school, and junk like that.

Then she goes off, and Mr. Chase appears after a while, and he's like a guy version of Mrs. Chase. I mean he shakes my hand and everything, like he's used to giving out business cards and remembering people's names. Brandon does the same deal with him, not making eye contact.

He really can't stand either one of them.

I can't see why. Maybe every kid has to hate their parents or something. It seems like the only thing I ever hear anybody say about their parents is griping, so it must be a teenager thing. That must be it.

Then Mrs. Chase calls us to eat, and I'm a little surprised because I thought the maid would serve the food and everything, but there's no maid around. It's just Mr. Chase, Mrs. Chase, Brandon, and me.

The table's big, and shiny, and all the plates and stuff match. Not only do they match each other, but they match the rug and the curtains. It's like a restaurant or something.

"Why don't you sit right there, Charlie?" says Mrs. Chase, so I do. Everybody's got a cloth napkin in a glass ring, and there's a couple of extra pieces of silverware by my plate, but I figure I'll just follow Brandon's lead.

Nobody says anything, but suddenly Mr. Chase starts talking. I notice Brandon's got his head bowed and I realize they're saying the blessing.

I kind of duck my head, out of respect, but I'm thinking how I almost wish I could belong in a place like this, where everything matches and there's a mother and father, and they pray together and everything.

Then Mr. Chase says, "Amen," and Brandon and his mom are saying, "Amen," but I'm too late, so I just kind of nod.

"So, Charlie," Mrs. Chase says as she hands me a platter of fish. "Are you enjoying the school year?"

"Yes ma'am." I figure I better stick with the polite stuff, until I get a definite message otherwise. I'm loading up my plate; everything looks good, like something out of a magazine. Even the fish has these little twirls of lemon all around it. I don't know if I'm supposed to take a twirl or not, so I don't.

"That's good. Are you doing all right in your classes?"

"Yes ma'am."

"Wonderful. You're planning on college, I hear."

"Yes," I say, to vary things up a little. "I am."

"TMU's a good school," says Mr. Chase. "Not Ivy League, of course, but a good, solid reputation." He hands me this humongous bowl of green things, and I swear to God they look like pickles. How the hell could somebody eat pickles for dinner? I put some on my plate anyway, to be polite.

Brandon hasn't said a word. He's just listening, and passing bowls around. He has some fish on his plate, and I check to see if *he* took a twirl. He didn't either, so that's all right.

"I hear you're in some of Brandon's advanced classes," Mrs. Chase says.

"Yes ma'am," I say, though I'm in exactly one of Brandon's classes, besides homeroom.

All the bowls have made the rounds, and Brandon picks up one of his forks, so I pick up mine, too. First thing I do is, I see if those things really are pickles. They're not. I don't know what they are, but they're not pickles. They don't really taste like anything at all.

"I haven't heard that you're involved in any extra-curricular activities," Mrs. Chase says. She says it like, *Tsk tsk*.

"No ma'am," I say.

"Time to start thinking about it," says Mr. Chase.

"It'll be good on scholarship applications," adds Mrs. Chase. When she says the word *scholarship,* her mouth pulls down and she looks at me, kind of sad.

"Sports are always good." Mr. Chase eyes me. "Football—well, you might make a receiver, if you can run. Not quite heavy enough for a lineman. Baseball might be better."

"You play golf, Mr. Chase?" I ask, because he's wearing a golfing shirt, and maybe if he gets off on golf everybody'll stop talking about me.

"Yes, I do. Three times a week. Been trying to teach Brandon, but he won't put in the practice time. Golf's not croquet, you know. It's a mental—"

"Now, dear," Mrs. Chase interrupts. "Charlie doesn't want to hear about golf." Under the dining-room light I can see that her hair's got about a ton of hairspray on it. "I hear your brother's raising you. *And* is working his way through college."

I look at Brandon, and he's looking at me like,

Don't blame *me*. And I don't. None of this is like top secret or anything, and his mom probably nagged it out of him anyway.

"By the way, Charlie," Mrs. Chase is saying, all sympathetic, "I was so sorry to hear your mother is no longer with us."

Why's she saying that, like it just happened? My mother has been dead what, six, seven years?

I don't know what to say. "Thank you?" "It's all right?" "No big deal?"

"I hope she didn't suffer?" Mrs. Chase says.

The way she says it makes me think maybe she's fishing to find out what my mother died from. Which means Brandon didn't tell her; he must have lied and said he didn't know.

I've got a choice, I can tell the truth and get pitied, or I can lie.

I don't like either choice.

"I'd rather not talk about it," I say. I take a bite of the fake pickles.

"Oh. Well." She doesn't know what to say about that, I guess nobody's told her that before. "We certainly wouldn't want to make you uncomfortable." She's smiling and then she gets all busy cutting her fish.

There's this silence for a moment, and then Mr. Chase clears his throat. "It's a nice change, having a little informal conversation. Isn't it, Brandon?"

"Yes sir," says Brandon. It's the first thing he's said since we sat down.

"You see, Charlie," Mr. Chase says, "most nights

we use mealtime to discuss topics of general interest. Politics, world events, that sort of thing. Broaden our horizons."

"You didn't get any zucchini, Brandon," Mrs. Chase says.

Mr. Chase looks around the table. He picks up the bowl of pickles. He doesn't hand it to Brandon, though. He just takes the spoon and plops a bunch onto Brandon's plate.

"Would you like some more, Charlie?" Mrs. Chase asks, smiling.

"No, thanks," I tell her. Mr. Chase puts the bowl down.

"You *are* going to eat, darling?" Mrs. Chase asks Brandon, and I notice he hasn't really eaten much. He's like a statue. An unhappy statue. And I can kind of see why.

Brandon doesn't touch his zucchini, and he doesn't answer his mom either. The silence kind of stretches out.

"Can I ask you something about golf?" I ask Mr. Chase. "It seems like one day it could be real windy, and the next day there might not be any wind at all. So how do you make the ball go where you want?"

"There's several adjustments you need to make," Mr. Chase says. He's off, talking about undercutting the ball and other shit I never heard of.

Mrs. Chase doesn't stop him this time, and after a while I kind of tune out. I mean, the guy goes on until the meal's practically over.

Then I see Mr. Chase is laying his napkin on the

table. He pushes his plate away. "I finally broke seventy the other day," he's saying. "In a tournament too. I always say, you can be good at anything, if you want it bad enough. Right, Brandon?"

"Yes sir. May we be excused?" Brandon asks. He doesn't wait for an answer, he just gets up, so I do too. He doesn't pick up his plate, so I don't either.

"Good dinner, Mrs. Chase," I tell her. "We don't do too much cooking at our place. More like defrosting."

"Well, you'll just have to come over more often then."

She's got this big smile. I don't know what the hell I did, but she likes me.

Brandon leads the way down a hall and through one of the living rooms and down another hall, and we're in his huge old cavern of a room, and he's shutting the door behind us.

"Sorry," is the first thing Brandon says.

"No big deal," I tell him. "Good food."

"I can't stand this place," he says. He's standing in the middle of the floor with his hands in his pockets, like he doesn't want to touch anything. I kind of walk around, looking at all his stuff. He's got trophies all over the place, and an aquarium with gravel and rocks and stuff that match the rest of the room.

"The minute I turn eighteen, I'm out of here."

"Where you going?" I'm bending over in front of the aquarium, looking for fish. I sure don't see any. Still, it looks good.

He doesn't answer right away, and when I glance over at him he's kind of eyeing me like he's weighing something out, in his mind.

He still doesn't say where he's going, but after a minute he goes over to the closet and pulls out that same file box I saw the other time. He brings it back over to the bed. "Nobody knows this," he says while he's turning the lock, and then he opens it.

I sit on the bed. The only thing in the box is books and papers, maybe a few pictures, and notes like you pass in school. "No booze," I say.

"I've cut back," Brandon says. "I'm not home much lately anyway." He's got his back to the door, and he's kind of sifting through the papers. He pulls out this sheet of paper that's all wrinkled and stained. He hands it to me.

It's a drawing, like a floor plan on the top, and the front of a house on the bottom. It's a log cabin, except it's too big for a cabin. It's like a home, a log home.

"Did you draw this?" I ask him. It looks like a place I wouldn't mind living.

"Yeah. One of these days I'm going to build it myself, somewhere in the mountains."

"Cool," I say, handing it back to him.

"Looks like shit, doesn't it?" It takes me a sec to realize he means the paper, not the drawing. "I had to dig it out of the trash. They're always throwing my stuff away. That's why I lock the important stuff up. Look at this." He pulls out another piece of paper and hands it to me.

It's some poem or something, it turns out to be about mountains. I'm betting Brandon wrote it, but I don't ask.

"Stoic trees—good image," I tell him, handing it back.

And that's the way it goes. Brandon hands me something out of the box and I look at it while he tells me about it.

He shows me school pictures, notes from girls, ticket stubs from movies he wasn't supposed to see. All kinds of stuff.

And I thought he hid his porno magazines in there.

The door opens as he's shutting the box.

It's Mrs. Chase. I get up kind of casual and walk over to the trophy shelves. I act like I'm looking at the trophies, just to deflect her attention from the bed.

"Charlie," she says without even giving Brandon a glance, "I bought these shirts for Brandon last month, but he's already got plenty. I'm pretty sure they'll fit you."

That's when I notice she's got all these clothes draped over her arm.

I'm just standing there by the shelves and it's like I can't move all of a sudden. My face is getting hot. Do I look that bad, like I need Brandon's rejects?

"Now, these shouldn't go in the dryer. And you'll need to wash them in cold, so they don't fade. Can you remember that?"

She holds them out, like she expects me to take them.

But I don't.

"Thanks," I say, "but I don't really need any clothes."

"It's all right. I know your brother must have a hard time making ends meet. And these have hardly been worn at all." She's eyeing my chest, and then she takes the top shirt and holds it up against my shoulders. "Trust me, they'll fit. You and Brandon are about the same size. Of course," she whispers, like she's sharing a secret, "they'll look better tucked in."

Then she gives me this little wink, and I don't have to look down to know that the shirt I'm wearing is *not* tucked in. It's practically flapping.

In a flash, I understand what Brandon was saying about his room that time, about specifications and how it wasn't really his. Because those shirts are someone else's taste and someone else's money and they aren't a gift, they come with instructions and rules and I bet if I took one and wore it tucked out, Mrs. Chase would get that sympathetic look and nag at me until I goddamn well tucked it in.

"No, thank you," I tell her, but I'm getting kind of mad.

"Mom," says Brandon.

"I'll just put them right here." Mrs. Chase drapes them over the chair at the desk. "Remember, hang dry, cold water—"

"And tucked in," adds Brandon, real low.

"Right." She smiles at him, or maybe she never stopped smiling. It's hard to tell. Anyway, she leaves.

Like it doesn't count if she doesn't *see* me take her charity. Fuck her. I leave the shirts hanging over the chair.

But damned if, when Brandon's getting ready to drive me home, she doesn't run after us to tap on the goddamn car window and hand me the whole pile.

I take them, just so she doesn't come up to school or something and stick them in my locker.

But as we're heading down Bellaire Drive, I buzz down the window and I throw every one of those shirts into the street.

I think I hear this gasp from Brandon's side of the car, but when I look around he's laughing. "I love it!" he says. "That's great."

It is kind of funny, I guess. So I take a deep breath, and when I let it out, I've managed to blow off Brandon's mom and dad. I can even smile back a little. I start noticing the big old houses we're passing. A lot of them have windows lighted and curtains open. It's like somebody's saying, *Take a look at all our stuff!*

I let myself wonder if Katie lives around here. Brandon's still kind of smiling to himself as he turns on the radio. It's that song by Alabama, about why's some guy rushing around all the time, when all he's really got to do is live and die.

"Want to cut through?" Brandon asks, and I realize he means cut through the residential neighborhood, past the house with the junky yard, I guess because it's night and maybe the guy won't recognize the car.

"No," I say. "What's the point?"

So we take the route past the soccer fields.

"Which do you think is worse?" Brandon asks, which means buckle in for one of his philosophical discussions. "Smacking a kid around or telling him he's not worth shit?"

I shrug.

"I think saying stuff is worse," Brandon states. "Hitting's over with. Words stay with you."

"I don't think so," I tell him. I usually don't get dragged in this early in the discussion, but he's got this all wrong.

Brandon turns the radio down. "Your mom ever hit you?" he asks.

"Some."

"Bad?"

I don't have that uncomfortable feeling in my chest I usually get whenever somebody asks about my mom. "Not too bad. No bruises. But one time my lip got busted open."

"What did Trent do?"

"Got in her face. Told her she'd better not ever touch me again."

"Did she?"

"No. But her drinking really went downhill after that." And it did too. All because just that once, I didn't see it coming.

"That wasn't your fault," Brandon says.

"No," I tell him, "it wasn't."

It's only the truth, but the funny thing is, it feels good to hear somebody else speak those words. Out loud. *It wasn't your fault, Charlie.*

"Did she ever say stuff?" Brandon asks.

139

"Some," I say.

"Like what?"

"Stupid. Lazy. Liar." Mom always went into more detail than that, but Brandon's got the idea.

"But you still think that's better than hitting?"

"Yeah," I tell him. "Because if it's not true, you don't have to listen."

Brandon shakes his head, and even though it's dark, I know he's smiling. "That's easy for you," he says. "You don't listen to anybody."

"Trent," I tell him. "I listen to Trent."

Brandon nods. He listens to Trent too.

"And you," I add.

"Me?" He sounds funny. Like, surprised or something.

"Yeah."

Up a little hill, then we're zipping toward my neighborhood.

"Hey," Brandon says.

I'm waiting, but he can't seem to get whatever it is out.

"I want to tell you something," he finally says, and his voice sounds kind of rusty. "You're the best friend I ever had."

Oh, man. I'm glad it's dark, so it's not like I have to *see* him going weird on me. "I guess we got some things in common," I say. I can't stand this emotional crap.

"Just about everything," Brandon says. "Sports. Philosophy. Sex."

"Can't ask for more than that," I say, watching the

140

houses go by. I'm wishing he'd lighten up. "Though I don't see you getting much in the way of sex lately."

"You're not kidding. Still, you got to give me credit for trying."

"The U.S. judge gives you a nine point nine," I tell him. I'm just glad the subject's changing.

But Brandon's not ready to change the subject. He's like Trent, once he decides he's going to say something, that's it. You've just got to grit your teeth and hold on till he gets it all out.

"You're the only person I really trust," he goes on, all serious. "You and Trent. Around y'all, I don't have to put on this big act and smile all the time." He's shaking his head. "If I feel like shit, I can just say so. It's weird. It's like the whole world's a total mess, and you and Trent are the only rock-solid, normal people I know."

"Man," I tell him, "if we're normal, the rest of the world's in deep trouble."

"I know you don't like to hear this kind of stuff," Brandon tells me, and boy, does he have that right. "All I'm trying to say is, if you ever need anything, I'm there. Trent too. Because you guys have been there for me."

I don't know what to say to that. So I just nod. And then, thank God, he shuts up.

But later on, when Trent's asleep and I'm in bed, I'm thinking about everything Brandon said. I figure I'd probably have to call him my best friend too.

But it's not that kind of sappy shit I'm thinking about. What I'm thinking about is that I've never actually mentioned to him that Trent's gay. At first I figured it wasn't any of his business. And then it just never seemed to come up in casual conversation.

But if I brought it up now, I'd feel stupid—because Chase has got to have picked up on it. It'll be like, Yeah, big news flash, Charlie, you moron.

Old Brandon's pretty sharp. He's seen that Trent never joins in when we're talking about girls. He's noticed that Trent's never said a word about his love life. Brandon understands that gays don't talk about stuff like that in front of straight guys. The way Brandon and I don't talk around girls the way we do when it's just us.

Everybody's got their compartments, I guess.

I'm getting kind of sleepy. I roll over onto my stomach, and I'm thinking about what we don't say around girls. I'm thinking if Misty knew half the comments Brandon's made about her tits, she'd slap the shit out of him.

CHAPTER 14

One Saturday in the middle of December Trent actually has the day off, and that morning the three of us go up to the P.E. building to work out. You're supposed to show a student I.D., but nobody ever hassles me or Brandon about getting in as long as we're with Trent.

As usual, we spend most of our time in the room with the free weights. When Brandon first started coming with us, he was more interested in the machines—you know, the ones with cables and pulleys and little keys that you stick in between the flat plates. Trent and I used to kid him how machines were for wimps—just up and down, up and down, up and down, not like free weights where you've got to use your entire muscle to control and balance.

So today, like every other day, Brandon sticks to the free-weight room. It's the three of us, and the guys with quads like sides of beef and lats so wide their big old bulky arms won't hang down at their sides like normal people's.

On the way back in Trent's car, we pass this other

car all decorated with shoe polish and everything. You know, "Just Married" and that kind of crap.

And then, back at the apartment, old Brandon's getting all philosophical again.

"I figure I'll get married when I'm like thirty or something," he says. We're sitting on the couch loading up on water. Rehydrating, as Trent says. "That'll give me plenty of time to play around, live a little. You know?"

"I don't even think that far ahead," I tell him. "Anything could happen between now and then."

"What about you, Trent?" Brandon asks. "You ever been serious about anybody?"

Trent's in the kitchen. He doesn't answer right away. He's thinking.

I'm thinking too. I'm thinking, what "anybody" does he mean?

Trent glances at me before he answers Brandon. He's never told Brandon either, I guess.

Of course not. He'd leave it up to me.

"Yeah, I have," Trent tells Brandon.

I get up. "Let's go shoot some baskets," I say. It comes out a little too loud. I don't know why, but I'm feeling like maybe I ought to get Brandon alone, just the two of us. "All this talk about getting serious is making me nervous," I tell them.

Brandon laughs. "You can practically feel the leash slipping around your neck." He acts like he's being choked, and Trent grins and shakes his head while I go to get my basketball.

As I'm walking into my room, I hear Brandon say to Trent, "You're twenty-four, aren't you?"

"Yeah."

"You think you'll ever get married?"

He *doesn't* know. All this time, and he still doesn't know.

I throw open the closet door, looking for my basketball. It's under a clean shirt.

"I don't plan on getting married," Trent finally says.

How stupid could Chase be? All the things that Trent's never said—how could Brandon not have a clue?

I take the shortcut back, jumping over the bed.

"That doesn't sound too bad, either," I hear Brandon say, and then I'm walking into the living room with my basketball under my arm. "But I might want a kid someday. I can't decide."

I scoop up our jackets from the back of the couch.

"You've got plenty of time to decide," Trent tells him.

"Come on," I tell Brandon, tossing him his jacket. As we're leaving, I give Trent a look, so he knows I'm going to take care of this.

Across the street at the middle school, I watch Brandon practicing his layups. It's a little cold, just standing there, so I pull the zipper of my sweat jacket all the way up. I'm thinking what to say.

The ball thunks against the backboard, then drops through the net. He's hit every one so far.

Now I'm feeling a little stuffy. I unzip my jacket. No words are coming into my head.

Brandon makes another run at the basket. Again, he nails it.

A breeze catches the sides of my jacket, pulling it apart. I tug the zipper halfway up and leave it there. "Hey, Chase," I say. "Trent's gay." Now *that's* tactful, isn't it?

"Yeah, sure," he says, dribbling back into position. This time, though, he takes the ball in both hands and plants his feet.

"No, really," I tell him. "He is."

"No he's not." Brandon bounces the ball a few times, getting a fix on the basket. "I spent the night at your place, remember?" he adds, and then he shoots. The ball sails up. It taps the backboard and falls gently through the net.

I don't see what spending the night has to do with anything. He's not listening or something.

So when he gets the basketball and comes back, dribbling slowly, like he's going to start the whole production again, I step over and take the ball out of his hands. Now he'll have to pay attention.

"Brandon," I say, holding the basketball. Looking right at him. "He is."

I figure he's going to take the ball back. But he doesn't, he's just standing there, with his arms dangling at his sides.

And this *look* comes over his face.

Cold. Almost . . . disgusted.

He doesn't say another word. He just jerks around, kind of shaky, like his muscles aren't getting the whole message from his brain. He starts walking back toward the apartments.

Okay, so we're finished shooting baskets. "I figured you already knew," I say as I catch up with him.

Brandon just keeps walking.

"Hey," I say, putting my hand on his shoulder so he'll slow down for a sec, *"listen."*

He flinches and knocks my hand away. Like he can't get out from under it fast enough.

But he does stop.

"I'm sorry," I tell him, which is once more than I've ever apologized to anybody in my life. "I really thought you knew."

He's staring at the ground now, and I can see he's definitely taking it in, and I'm kind of holding my breath, because now that he's taking it in, he's got to realize that not telling him wasn't anything personal.

"Jesus." He spits the word out. "I changed clothes at your place today." He raises his head, he's looking at me now—like I tried to force him to eat shit for breakfast or something. "God. Right in *front* of him."

"What diff—"

"I took off my fucking *clothes!*" The last word comes out as a shout. He starts backing away. "Shut up!" he tells me, although I didn't say anything. He turns around, and he keeps walking. "Just shut up," I hear him say again, and it's like he's still trying to

147

shout, but his voice comes out all smashed and mangled.

And now I can see that he's not heading back to the apartment. He's heading toward the parking lot. Toward his car. I can't believe it.

He doesn't stop walking, but I do.

He's crossing the street, and then he's disappearing around the corner, and after a few moments I hear the engine turn over. And then he's gone.

I still can't believe it. I'm just standing there, holding the ball. It's not sinking in. It's like I can't feel anything. It's like everything's numb.

I think I take the ball and dribble it around a little, but I'm not really aware of what I'm doing. I know I shoot, and I know I miss. And I know I pick up the ball and go home.

CHAPTER 15

Trent's sitting at the table working on some home-work when I walk in. He looks up when I slam the door. I didn't mean to, it just slipped out of my hand.

"He didn't take it too well," Trent guesses.

I don't say anything.

"I'm sorry," Trent says, and he sounds like he means it.

I don't feel like hearing it. I don't feel like hearing much of anything, to tell the truth. I can see the courtyard, through the sliding glass door, and I'm so tired all of a sudden, I want to lay my forehead against the glass and shut my eyes, but I don't. I just kind of lean against the wall, looking outside.

"You were wrong," I say. "All that crap about liv-ing in a box. You know what happens when you open yourself up? You get kicked in the face."

"Charlie—" Trent starts.

"So much for your stupid ideas," I tell him.

Trent's all quiet. Then he shrugs and bends over his book again. He's trying to ignore me.

I notice I'm still holding the basketball under my

arm. I hurl it across the room. It bounces off the wall and bangs into the end table, knocking the lamp over.

I can feel Trent watching me. Real steady. Like I did something wrong.

Which I did. I listened to him.

"None of this would have happened if you weren't a pervert," I point out. I don't really think that, I've never felt that. But right now it's like there's something hurting me really bad inside, so bad that I can't look at it, not even while it stabs its way out.

"A pervert?" Trent repeats, like he can't believe I said that. Like I just kicked *him* in the face.

"Per-vert," I say, very clearly.

Trent's staring at me like he's just met me for the first time. And the first impression really sucks. "Well, I probably am, to *you*." He pushes back his chair and gets up, real deliberate. "*I* generally know the last names of people I sleep with," he announces.

I don't see what that has to do with anything. And I can't stand Trent when he gets sarcastic.

"I even actually care about them first—What an idea! Having feelings for somebody before you drop your pants!"

I just kind of stare at him. So he can see to back off.

"Not having a *feel,* having feel*ings.* Like, emotion? Can you say that, Charles? E-mo-tion."

I don't answer. I'm getting kind of pissed.

"*I* don't hide out, refusing to take phone calls from a girl I've been screwing for months. *I* don't take some stranger's virginity like she's offered me a Kleenex. You, on the other hand, take sex about as seriously as blowing your nose," he tells me, like he's made some big point or something.

"Fuck you," I tell him, because I'm too mad to think of anything else to say.

"Now *there's* an intelligent comment. What rapier-like wit, Charles. Any more stunning remarks?"

I swear to God, if it wasn't Trent, I'd kill him.

But Trent's mad too, even though he isn't yelling, and he's not finished. "You wouldn't know a relationship if it bit you on the ass," he says in this perfectly even voice. "You behave like an animal."

Now I'm ready to kill him.

"Somebody *ought* to lock you up in a box."

Then I'm coming at him like a tank, and I've got him all slammed up against the wall. He doesn't make any move to defend himself, he's not even hitting me, and I can't bring myself to hit him, so I just grab the front of his shirt and I want to yell at him but I don't know what to yell.

I'm just holding these handfuls of shirt all scrunched up, and I don't know what to do, because Trent's never said anything like that to me before, and I can't forget the surprise on his face when I mowed into him. So I just kind of glare at the front of his shirt and pound my fists on his chest, but not hard, almost like he's not even there.

"Charlie," I hear him saying, "God. I'm sorry. I'm so fucking sorry," and he must really be in some weird mood, because he almost never talks like that. "I wish everything could be . . . I wish you never had to deal with . . . you're my *brother,* man . . ." His voice kind of tightens up, and he doesn't finish.

I shut my eyes for a second, and it's like I'm on the edge of something, of going insane or sobbing or putting my fist through a wall. Then I open my eyes, and it's just Trent, and he's looking at me like *I'm* the one who's hurt, not him. And I see that I'm mashing him against the wall, so I open my fists and let his shirt go. Then I step back, and I kind of nod to let Trent know I'm okay, and then I walk outside, because all of a sudden it's too fucking quiet in here.

I don't know where I go, I jog, I walk, and for once I don't go sit by the pool and look at the water because it's too close and I have to keep moving.

At one point I'm down by the soccer fields and I look around and I'm thinking it's too bad you can't tell who hates gays, just by looking at them. It'd save a lot of trouble.

Boy, did I blow it. Not because I was stupid enough to think he'd figure it out on his own, but because I was stupid enough to almost let myself care what somebody else thought.

I'm sitting on the dead leaves and grass down by the creek, and I'm thinking, What business is it of anybody's what Trent does when he's not around them? I mean, does that fuckwad Chase sit around and dwell on what his parents do in their bedroom? I know I sure as hell wouldn't.

It sounds like he thinks Trent's been secretly lusting after him or something. Like he's so irresistible.

And he should know Trent better than that, anyway.

I'm sitting on the dried-up grass, and I'm kind of tearing out handfuls of it, and I'm thinking, Why does this shit happen to me? I mean, all those years in East Texas I couldn't make friends because you never knew what my mom would say or do, or how other kids would react to it. It was best to just stay apart.

But I'd watch other kids, and how it seemed so easy for them to go to each other's houses and to talk to each other all the time, and part of me was almost glad when my mother died. Because I thought it was like magic, now I'd be like everybody else.

But it wasn't magic. Somehow in all those years I missed learning how to do all the stuff that comes to Brandon so easily—talking to people I don't know, opening up to them, that kind of crap. All the stuff that comes so easily to everybody except me.

And then when I do try to learn, what happens?

I get kicked in the face.

I lie back in the grass and think about it for a while. I figure maybe other people had to open up a lot of times for it to come so easy. Maybe everybody started when they were little, and they've like built up an immunity so it doesn't bother them anymore.

I think some more, and then I get up and start

walking home. It's a long walk from here, but I'm calm now and tired enough that there aren't any feelings getting in my way.

I've decided that I'm not little anymore. It's too late, for me.

I'm walking along the creek bed, not really wanting to head up into the world of cars and people and apartments.

The terrible thing is, now I can see how somebody would want to shut themselves up and never go out. And now I can see how somebody would take to drinking, if they were already inclined to do that sort of thing.

Anything to shut up the quiet that you know you'll always be alone with.

I'm just kind of walking along, kicking at some grass. For the first time . . . almost, kind of, sort of . . . I can understand my mom.

CHAPTER 16

When I get back, Trent doesn't say another word about what happened—which is a little unusual. And he doesn't go out that night, he stays home and watches reruns of *Baywatch* with me. Which is strange too.

But what's downright weird is he doesn't make fun of it at all. Not one joke about slow-motion silicone or seventh-grade scriptwriters. He just sits there on the couch, like this is his all-time favorite show or something.

But I don't ask any questions. Because I don't want to get him started talking.

On Sunday, I sleep late while Trent goes to work. When I do get up, I spend the day eating crap and watching garbage on TV.

That evening, when Trent gets home, he doesn't ask what's for supper. He takes one look at me and tells me I'm getting flabby from sitting around all day and I'm going up to the P.E. building to work out with him, like it or not.

I get the feeling Trent's hoping I'll argue. Hoping I'll tell him to piss off and leave me alone.

But I don't feel like arguing. I just say okay.

Only we walk up to the building and it turns out the whole place is locked up. There's a sign on the door that says the electricity's off.

Trent's got his weight-lifting gloves in one hand, his towel in the other. "Damn," he says, slapping the towel against his thigh. He's an exercise addict. "Maybe we should wait and see if they get it back on."

"They might not," I say.

"We could go run." Trent's all primed, and here he is being denied his workout.

"Or," I point out, "we could just go home."

Trent's been eyeing the building like he might just scale it and go in through the roof, but when I say that he stops and looks at me. "You really don't feel like doing this, do you?" he says.

I shrug.

"All right," he finally says, looking at the sign like it's some insult aimed at him personally, "I guess I'll have to risk losing my six-pack." He pats his stomach and gives me a grin.

It's a joke. Trent works like a dog on his abdominal muscles, but he can't seem to get that washboard look, like some of the super-beefy guys. Genetics, I guess—or maybe steroids.

I don't smile. I just put my towel around my neck, ready to go home.

Trent stops smiling. He's all quiet for a minute, just watching me.

"I've been thinking," he says.

156

Uh-oh.

"Everybody's had a bit of a shock this weekend. And everybody's overreacted—me included."

I don't say anything. I kind of frown off into the distance, so he'll know he can lay off anytime now.

"Everybody's said and done things they regret."

"You ready to go?" I ask.

"I've been thinking about Brandon," Trent announces.

"Good for you," I say. I turn away, to head back to the car.

But Trent's coming with me, all casual, like I didn't just walk away from him. I can't believe I didn't see this coming. He's got a bug up his butt that's been building since yesterday, and now he's going to talk this thing to death.

"I figure," Trent says, "as far as Brandon knows, gay guys are flits in spandex molesting young boys. And here he's gotten close to me and actually liked me. It probably shook him up." I'm walking pretty fast, but he's just strolling along like he planned it that we'd be walking back to the car at this exact moment, discussing this exact thing. "Because, you know, virginity can weigh on a guy."

I don't know what virginity's got to do with anything. I just keep walking.

"Brandon's never had sex, and you know how it is. It's stupid, but it's like you're never really positive you're going to be able to do it, until you've done it just once."

In a flash, I understand what Trent's getting at.

I can't help it, I stop. Right in the middle of the parking lot, next to a Toyota pickup. "You think Brandon's gay?" I ask.

"No," says Trent. "I think he's *scared*. I think it crossed his mind that maybe he is but doesn't know it—and it scared him. And I think he's even more scared what other people might think."

I don't say anything. I remember all of a sudden how it used to cross my mind, when I was in middle school, that maybe I was too. But I didn't come all unglued, I just thought it out and realized I wasn't attracted to guys.

"What a wuss," I say, kind of disgusted.

Trent's staring at me. Then he just kind of throws his head back and laughs.

"God, Charlie," he says. "Sometimes you stun me with your sensitivity."

"What?" I ask. I spot Trent's car, on the other side of the pickup. I start walking again. "He *is* a wuss. Nick didn't shit bricks when he found out you were gay."

"Nick was pretty hard-nosed." Trent kneels to dig his car key out of his sock. I know he doesn't mean anything bad. Trent liked Nick. "You couldn't shock that kid with thirty thousand volts. I'd bet that what Brandon's going through isn't much different from what anybody else goes through. He's just led a shel-tered life. So he's got to hit the wall a little harder, that's all."

"Boo-hoo," I say. I'm ready to tell Trent I don't give a shit how hard Brandon hits any walls.

Then it hits me, I'm talking about it.

"I'm not going to talk about this anymore," I tell him over the roof of the car. He glances at me as he unlocks the door, and I guess he knows I mean it, because he doesn't say another word.

Which is almost too bad, because I didn't get a chance to mention what I've figured out, over this long weekend.

If you know when to cancel out, you won't get dragged down and you won't get hurt.

So it's like the whole Chase episode never happened. From that first tap on the shoulder, to the scene on the basketball court—I've canceled it all out.

—— CHAPTER 17 ——

Monday morning I'm cutting through the front foyer before school. Brandon's standing in that big circle of people like always, but who cares? I'm not going to stop.

I just head for the library to turn in my book.

"Hey, Calmont!" somebody yells. I glance over as I'm walking. Big mistake.

It's Luke Cottington. "I hear your brother's a fag," he says, loud and clear.

Anger roars over me. My legs are still walking so I turn my face back to the library and don't even stop. The anger's this hot wave trying to blast out, blast Chase and Cottington and their whole fucking crew.

I don't let it show. I just open the door and go in.

But after I'm in the library, after I've dropped the book in the slot and the worst of the hot wave has rolled on, I hesitate.

It hits me—if I just stay in here till the bell rings, I won't have to walk by those bastards again.

It lasts only a split second, but I can't stand that the thought even crossed my mind. I've never hated anything the way I hate myself for letting that split second happen.

So I get my legs going, and I walk out, under control, not dreading. Just a body, walking. Past Cottington and his buddies.

And Chase, who's just standing there staring down at the floor, like he didn't just put my brother up for target practice. That son of a bitch.

"Is it true?" Luke says, coming right up in my face, so I have to stop. He's enjoying this. "Your brother likes boys?"

I should have kept walking right through him. Because I'm standing there, and there's nothing I can say.

I'm not going to lie and say "No." If I say "Yeah," it'll be open season on Trent. And if I say "None of your goddamn business," it'll be an invitation to hear this same crap every day for the rest of my life.

I can't win. It feels like I'm stuck in cement with the anger boiling up inside, because I don't know what to do.

The place is like still. Waiting for a fight, I guess. Everybody's all standing around, watching and listening. And nobody, including Brandon Chase, says a thing.

"Does it run in the family?" says Luke, real loud.

My mouth wants to say "Fuck you," but I figure that's not such a good thing to say right now.

Brandon's still got his eyes on his shoes, like he's ashamed or something. But he's not too ashamed to listen. And he's not ashamed enough to say anything. Why should he? Why should he help *me* out?

"I hear it's genetic," Luke's saying, all fake-sincere, you know, where he knows everybody's listening to him and watching him have his fun.

I could hit him, easy. But I'll get suspended because it's a second offense. And it'll be like I think being gay is something to be ashamed of.

And if I hit him, he'll know he's getting to me.

"You like boys, Calmont?" Luke asks, just that little bit too loud.

"Charlie likes girls."

It cuts into the silence, it's a girl's voice, and it surprises Luke and me enough that we both look around.

Katie. I haven't talked to her at all, not since she came to my locker, and I didn't see her standing there with the others. God, she's pretty, all smooth-skinned and soft-haired. I remember how soft.

She hasn't moved, she's just holding her books all casual, like she's just mentioned what time it is.

"How would you know?" sneers Luke.

Bad move.

"I know," she tells him. From ten feet away. Loud and clear.

She *does* know, but she can't say what I think she's going to say. Not in the front foyer in front of every guy that's ever dreamed of an easy lay. She wouldn't say it out loud. Would she?

"How do you know?" Luke asks Katie again, and he's standing perfectly still, and his face is like a mask.

"Remember Misty's party? Remember Charlie and I went for a walk?"

Luke remembers, all right. A muscle in his jaw starts twitching.

Katie's watching Luke, all steady, and her face is like a mask now, too. Not like that night, when she was so serious, trying to see sparkles and shadows in the water. Not at all like later, when her face was right beneath mine and her hands were in my hair.

"Katie—" It's the first time I've called her by her name, but she doesn't even blink.

"We didn't just *walk,*" she tells Luke.

All or nothing. All for me, nothing for Luke.

Luke's pissed, boy, is he pissed, he's going to explode. If he touches Katie, I'll kill him.

He flings his books clear across the foyer and as they hit the glass trophy cases with this huge bonging sound he's stalking away.

I notice my hands are starting to cramp, and then I notice it's because they're in fists.

The next thing I notice is that I'm not angry anymore.

I unclench my hands. Luke's papers are fluttering to the ground, and everything's very quiet. It's so quiet I almost feel like laughing.

I don't look at Brandon at all. I do meet Katie's eyes—she's got more balls than anybody in this place—and then I can't help it, I do laugh a little, and then my body starts walking and suddenly the world starts getting noisy again, people move and talk, like they couldn't do anything until I released them.

163

* * *

Okay, so my book's dropped off.

I walk down the hall. Around the corner. Down the next hall. And then I'm heading into my first-period class—the same way I do every other day of the world.

It's as if those few moments in the front foyer never took place.

No one else is in algebra yet. The room is neat and sharp like always—the desks lined up on the square tiles, the papers at right angles on the bulletin board. Ms. McGuiness is pretty factual, she doesn't go in for perking up the place with smiley faces or anything.

I take out my pencil and my assignment sheet, and I walk over to stand in front of the bulletin board to copy the assignment down before the bell rings. Like I always do.

I'm only a few feet from the door, so when there's footsteps, and this blur of denim and white coming in, I don't have to look around to see who it is.

It's Chase.

I hear him walk over to his desk and put his books down. The silence kind of stretches out. I keep writing.

"I won't be able to give you a ride home," I hear him say.

Looks like we're having a quiz today.

"Hey," he says, like I argued with him. "All I did was tell the truth. I got plastered with Cottington, and I told him the truth. Is that some big crime?"

Page 94, I write. *1–9 odd.*

"At least *I* told the truth," Brandon says, and I don't even hear how he's all breathless and angry-sounding, "You both presented me with this big *lie.*"

Page 96. 1–15 all.

"You got anything else you want to spring on me? Like maybe you're both convicted murderers?"

I'm just checking to make sure I'm getting the right page numbers.

I hear him walk over and pull the classroom door shut, right beside me. "Okay," he says, real low. "So maybe telling Luke wasn't the brightest thing I've ever done."

He's saying this, and I'm trying not to listen, but it's kind of hard when we're the only two people in the room, and he's talking right at the side of my head.

"You know I liked him okay, before."

He can't even say Trent's name. Like Trent really *is* a murderer.

"It's just, all of a sudden, he's not that guy. Who I was friends with."

So what, I'm thinking. Why doesn't the bell ring?

"All right," Brandon says, kind of tight. "Fine. I'm sorry I told Cottington. Is that what you want? I'm *sorry.* Okay?"

I feel like some dog's waiting, going to hang around forever to see if I'll hand him a biscuit.

I won't.

I turn my head to face him. I look him right in the

165

eye. "Ask me if I give a shit," I tell him. Canceled out. Feeling nothing.

Then I turn back to the bulletin board, and I'm not even thinking how Chase's eyes were maybe starting to blur up a little.

I'm just trying to find where I left off copying. Because somehow I lost my place.

The bell rings.

Chase is going back over to his desk. I hear him scoop up his stuff, and then he's breezing past again. "Go fuck yourself," I hear him say. Bangs the door open, and then he's gone.

The door's still open. People start coming in.

I finally figure out I've already copied down everything I need. So I go sit in my desk, and keep my head down to study for the quiz.

It's funny, how easy it's turned out to be—canceling everything out.

CHAPTER 18

All the rest of the day, some of the friends of Brandon the Barometer kind of back off being friendly to me. The others, who make a big point of still saying hi to me in the halls—well, I just don't answer. I never said it first anyway.

At three-thirty the final bell rings and I head out of class, like I always do. I'm walking up to my locker, and I hardly even notice that Brandon, Luke, and David happen to be down by their lockers.

Some upperclass jocks are passing by, on their way to the rich-guy parking lot. "Hey, Cottington," I hear one of them call. "That the guy who porked the love of your life?"

He's talking about me, I guess.

Luke doesn't say anything. I don't know why, but I glance at him. He's just standing there in front of his locker, looking kind of pissed and miserable.

Brandon's next to him, at his own locker. I catch his eye for a second without really meaning to—he looks just plain miserable—but I don't dwell on it.

I'm just turning the combination dial so I can

dump my books off. I don't particularly feel like doing homework tonight.

"So," Luke says suddenly, loud, as I open my locker door and toss my books in the bottom. "I'll bet Calmont's brother brings his meat home."

Carlson gives one little bark of laughter.

"Let it go, Cottington," I hear Chase say. He sounds tired.

I try to shut my locker, but the door bounces open again. The corner of one of my folders is sticking out. I give it a nudge with my toe, but it won't go back in.

"That way Calmont gets to select the choice cuts," I hear Luke say.

I kick the folder, but that one corner pops right back out. Only now it's crinkled and bent.

"Because," Luke goes on, "he can't re*sist* a well-done T-bone."

He says it *lisping*.

I bend down to straighten the folder with my hand. My chest is getting tight inside. The muscles, or something.

"He prefers his meat tenderized," Luke says, still in this exaggerated lisp, like that's what gays really sound like.

"Leave him alone," Brandon says, kind of strained. But Carlson's snickering.

"Basted in its own juice," says Luke, and he's laughing too, but he still manages to sound like some prancing cartoon character.

Now everything's nice and neat. In the locker, I

168

mean—my body's doing weird things. The blood's pounding in my head, through my chest, into my arms. Pounding. Pounding.

I stand up. I shut the locker.

"Hey, Printh Charlth," Luke calls. "Taythed any thirloin lately?"

I start walking. Like I always do. Heading down the hall. Away from the rich-guy parking lot.

"Shut up, Luke." Brandon spits the words as I'm crossing the ten feet between the lockers. "For once in your life, just shut up."

"What?" Cottington spits right back. He doesn't notice I'm six feet away. "You develop a little taste for A.1. yourself, Chase?"

Silence. Two feet away.

"No," says Brandon, flat and angry, and I'm right behind them, I'm just walking down the hall, like I always do.

And I *am* going to pass them. I really am.

I don't know what goes wrong. I'm just kind of thinking about Trent singing "Happy Birthday" in the doorway, and how his voice is actually pretty deep, not high and lispy like Luke's goddamn cartoon voice, and somehow my hand reaches out as I'm passing and as soon as it touches Luke's back I'm putting my whole shoulder into it.

Boom! Cottington slams face-first into the lockers.

And before he can shake it off and turn around, I'm on him.

Luke's not giving up, he's kind of twisting around,

but still I manage to bang his face into the metal shelves a couple of times before he gets a hand up behind him. He blindly grabs a handful of my hair.

Luke fights like a goddamn *girl.*

I'm thinking this, and it's funny how I don't feel anything at all. It's like I'm watching some other guy trying to grind Luke Cottington into the floor.

I've got hold of Luke's arm and I don't care if he rips my scalp off, I've got his shirt too, all twisted up, and I'm crushing him into the locker. Not nice and clean, because I'm half in the way myself. It's ugly and we're both squirming and panting and grunting. But I don't care, I don't care if blood's running in his eyes. I have to smash that asshole Cottington's face into the metal, even if he's trying to pull me around to where he can shove *me* into the locker.

Hands are on me, trying to pull me away. Maybe they've been there for a long time. Maybe they've only been there a few seconds. "Charlie." It's Brandon's voice, almost in my ear, urgent. "They're com—"

I jab my elbow backward, without looking. It connects, and the hands are gone.

"Hey! Hey!" a man's voice is shouting, and something—a knee or a shoulder or maybe both—wedges itself between me and Cottington.

Or tries to. Because Cottington and I are like sewn together or something. It's because my hands won't let go, of his shirt, of his arm.

The sound of ripping cloth, and Cottington's being jerked away from me.

I'm still panting. I'm just standing there, and

Luke's across from me, and blood is running down his forehead, and his nose is beet red and bleeding from one nostril, but still he's glaring like he'd like to kill me, except he's being held back by a shop teacher.

"You all right, Luke?" It's a man's voice, and I don't really look around, because it's starting to occur to me that there's about a million people looking on—that audience that always comes crawling out from behind the baseboards whenever there's a fight.

But then it also occurs to me that the voice belongs to Mr. Payton. So I have to look.

He's scanning the scene, and you can see he's getting everything mapped out in his mind. Who's going down, and who's just in the way. His eyes flick right over me and land on Luke again.

"Yeah," Luke's answering.

"I think we'd better see if we can catch the nurse," Mr. Payton tells him. "Just to be on the safe side."

"I'm okay," Luke insists. He swipes his nose with the back of his hand.

Payton ignores him. "Would you escort Mr. Cottington to the nurse's office?" he asks the shop teacher. "Luke, when you're finished there, stop by my office."

And then—maybe because Luke's face is all bloody, maybe because I was winning when they came along or because I wouldn't let go, or maybe because Luke's Mr. Baseball Star—for whatever reason, Payton grabs my arm, up high, like you'd grab a little kid who's stepped off the curb too quick.

I jerk my arm away. If he touches me again, I'll kill him.

Payton's hand freezes in midair. I guess I broke some holy law or something. His eyes are locked on to me, over the rim of his glasses.

I stare back, eye to eye.

Nobody's making a sound.

Payton lowers his hand.

"Let's go," he says. Two words. A hammer driving a nail. *Whack, whack.*

Looks like I just made him mad.

We start walking. As I'm passing, Cottington tugs his shirt down, smoothing out the spots where I twisted it.

Carlson's pretending to be part of the audience, come to watch.

Brandon stands a little apart from the others. He's breathing hard, and the area around his left eye's kind of red—maybe that's what my elbow hit. His shirt's not tucked in anymore.

I glance at him, kind of curious, as we get closer. To see if he's feeling it too, this strange numbness that's dropped down over the school like a blanket.

He's not. Something's going on with him, and something about his expression is very familiar—but I don't have time to think about it, because I'm being escorted down the hall like a convicted murderer or something.

*   *   *

When we're inside the office, Payton actually kicks the door shut with his foot.

I just look at him.

"Have a seat," he says. *Whack, whack, whack.*

I don't say anything. But I don't sit down either. I'm staring at him. I guess you'd call it glaring, if I was mad. But I'm not mad. I'm not anything at all.

He doesn't walk around his desk, he doesn't make a move to go get my card. He just stands there, looking somewhere in the direction of my knees. He draws a deep breath, lets it out real slow—like, Don't kill the kid, you'll get sued.

"What's the matter with you?" he finally says, but it's not really a question.

So I don't answer.

"Did you see what you did to that boy's face?"

I don't even shrug. This whole thing is stupid, a waste of time. It's obvious what's going to happen. Cottington'll get off with OCS—at worst. Maybe he'll get off with nothing, because he's all beat up. Me, I'm going to get suspended because it's a second offense.

And Trent's going to find out everything that happened today.

"You were in here at the beginning of the year," Payton says.

Don't ask me how he remembers. All those infractions, and I'm the one he remembers. Maybe all the others were like the same ten guys, rotating.

Payton folds his arms like, It's after three-thirty and I don't get overtime to deal with your shit.

I stare back at him.

"Do you come out swinging every time you have a problem?" he asks.

I don't say anything. Somewhere, deep inside, my chest is starting to ache.

"Isn't that what happened at the beginning of the year? You came out swinging?"

I don't *want* to say anything. My throat is getting tight, so tight it feels like I swallowed a burr.

"You think busting noses and fracturing skulls is going to win you a bunch of friends?"

God, does he have it all wrong.

"Fuck this," I croak. I actually say it out loud—I say the F-word, and then I'm turning to leave. I'm going to get suspended anyway, right? No way I'll stand here and listen to this over-the-hill loser who doesn't know his head from his ass.

"Sit down!" booms Mr. Payton as I reach the door. "I'm not finished with you yet."

I grab the knob anyway, and I turn it.

And then I'm out of this hole where everybody's in your face and nobody will just leave you the hell alone.

Brandon looks up, surprised. He's sitting in the corridor, in one of the orange plastic chairs right out-side the door.

His mouth opens as I'm barreling past, but if any words come out, they fade before they can follow me, because I'm already gone.

Down the hall, past the glass walls and the stupid

174

front foyer. And then I'm bursting through the heavy doors into the open air.

I jump down the steps. The orange bricks seem to be breathing at my back. All of it's breathing at my back. The friendships and the backstabbing and that goddamn cartoon lisp. The phone Payton's going to use to call Trent at work.

I'm running, I guess, because I can feel the concrete sending shock waves against the soles of my feet. Down the sidewalk, across Berry Street—brakes squeal, a horn blares somewhere not too far from my left thigh—but I'm still running.

I don't slow down until I remember there's no place to go.

I'm way past Berry now. I'm on one of those residential streets, marked with potholes, lined with perky little houses that trolls or dwarves might live in.

My feet have eased down to a walk. It's very quiet. There's no cars or people because it's the middle of the afternoon. I feel like I'm walking on a movie set, like I'm the only living thing here.

The whole day's been like a movie, where you're sitting in the dark watching things happen on a screen, and nothing touches you because it doesn't really have anything to do with your life.

I happen to glance down as I step up on a sidewalk, and I catch a glimpse of something red. I keep walking, though, even as I'm seeing that there are little drops of blood on my shirt. Cottington's blood, I guess. I don't think I got hurt. If I did, I don't feel it.

I'm glad to be numb. I'd hate to think what a guy would have to feel, to bash Cottington's face in like that.

The yards I'm passing are tight with silence. The empty windows are still. And all of a sudden I realize where my feet are taking me.

They're taking me to the kid's house.

It's up ahead now, every bit as junky as it was back in August, but the weeds are even higher, even if they are brown now. I can't see the kid yet—and I know there's no way he'll be waiting there on the tricycle, not after all this time.

I know he won't, but my heart is beating like I'm still at a full sprint.

Because if he *is* there, I get the feeling I might go right up to him and stop. For the first time, I might stop—because that kid has to live in an asylum of a house every day, afraid to talk and run and play. And when he gets bigger, school's going to be an even bigger asylum where you get screwed if you don't have two parents who lope up there at the drop of a hat to get you out of trouble.

The kid's whole life is totally fucked even before he's started it. And there's nothing he can do. Nothing.

I don't know why, but I just want to stop for a second. Just for a second—I don't know why.

But as I get closer and closer, I can see that there's no little blond head turned to look for me. Just the empty sidewalk, peeking half-choked out of the dead weeds.

Of course he's not there. It was pretty stupid to think he might be.

My feet slow down, anyway. They stop right there, on the old cracked sidewalk.

I'm exactly where the kid used to wait. Not facing the street, though. I'm facing that house. I never really looked at it much before. But today I do. I've never been in it—but still I know what it's like inside.

Bare wooden floors, water-stained paint, cracks edging their way up the wall from the corners of the doorways. Registers in the floors, chipped paint on the windowsills. In the kitchen, curled-up linoleum, peeling wallpaper, a faucet missing a handle.

I know because I lived in it. Maybe not this exact house, in this exact town, but I lived in it.

In some ways, it looks like I'll always live in it.

The tightness clutches at my throat again. I turn away, to leave.

And that's when I see it, in the weeds off the sidewalk.

The tricycle. Red and rusted. In the exact same position it was the day the bulldog guy flung it, the day Brandon and I drove off down the street.

Nobody's touched it since that day.

The handlebars are still twisted around, like a broken neck. The left rear wheel's still sticking up all useless in the air. The weeds are rising through the spokes like all they need is a good hold and they're going to drag the whole thing down till nobody'll ever see it again.

I'm the only one who knows. This rusted tangle of

bars and spokes—I'm the only one who knows it used to sit out here on the concrete, all shiny and red, and a little blond kid used to wait on it. Every day. For me.

The tightness grips higher. I feel it forcing my breath, quick and shallow. I feel it squeezing my face into stone. I feel it rising, right to the edges of my eyes.

I blink, to make it go away. It won't. It just clings there, on the edge.

And then it falls.

That's when I know. When I feel a couple of tears edging their way down my face, I finally admit what a moron I am.

I care about things. Too fucking many things. Things nobody can do anything about. The kid. Brandon. Katie. Being alone. Not having any friends.

And Luke's whiny cartoon lisp. God. I can take almost anything, but I can't take it when people who don't know Trent see him as less than he is. And *laugh*.

I wipe my face with the back of my arm. I remember I left my jacket at school, in my locker. It's cold, I really ought to go home now. I want to be there when Trent comes in, so all this doesn't hit him in the face. Because I know how much Trent does for me—he divides his life into two worlds, just so I don't have to face days like today.

But the thing is, Trent won't be there yet. He can't just leave work, he'll have to call somebody in to take over for him.

My hands are getting cold. I cram them down in the pockets of my jeans. I don't want to go home. Nobody'll be there. Nobody's waiting for me.

I notice I'm still standing where the kid used to sit on the trike. I turn around.

Then I squat down, to look out at the world the way he used to. Because I'm kind of wondering what he saw.

Nothing much. No cars coming. It's pretty quiet on this street, in the middle of the afternoon. Poor kid must have had a long wait, on his crappy little trike.

I'm looking down the street, and I can almost see it in my mind. A shining silver Corvette humming toward me. A window being buzzed down. Me, sitting in the front passenger seat. Ready to wave.

I'm feeling a lot of things I never felt before. Sick, for the little blond kid. Worried, about telling Trent. Amazed, at Katie, for going out on a limb in front of everybody. For being so decent to me, when the truth is that I wasn't all that decent to her.

I'm feeling that there's something that needs to be said, between me and Katie. I don't know what it is—I don't even know where to start.

All I know is that I ought to at least try.

I'm crouched down on the sidewalk, trying to figure all this out—and then I really *do* see it.

Down the street, a Corvette. Not shining; the sky's kind of overcast today. But silver, for sure.

I know it can't be Brandon. Brandon's got no reason to cut through this crappy neighborhood. Not anymore.

But here's this silver Corvette coming toward me, and for a second it's like I'm in a time warp or something. Because it's definitely headed this way.

It is Brandon. I stand up. I feel panicked, like I ought to run. Like I'm about to get some kind of death blow or something.

I don't move, though. I just jam my hands farther down into my pockets and stand there staring straight ahead like I'm waiting for a bus.

Chase pulls up right in front of me. He buzzes the passenger window down. He forgot his coat too. He leans over, peering up into my face. His eye is puffy now, and starting to darken. But all he says is:

"You okay?"

I'm looking at Brandon, and he's looking at me, and I don't have a clue what to say. *Am* I okay? I don't know—I think I might be. Because I can feel that last shred of tightness uncoiling. And for the first time in three days, I feel like I can actually breathe.

I don't know how to say that, though. I'm just standing there like a little kid, like a moron, like a basket case. I feel stupid as hell.

Finally, I just nod.

Brandon slumps back in his seat. I can't see his face anymore. He doesn't seem to know what to say either.

After a moment his voice comes from inside the Corvette, so low I can barely hear it over the drone of the engine.

"I'm sorry, man. I'm so fucking sorry."

Something about the way he says it echoes in my head. It's like I've heard those words before.

I'm sorry. I'm so fucking sorry.

And then it clicks. Those were Trent's words, after I slammed him into the wall.

And Brandon's expression, earlier—that was Trent's look. Like it didn't matter who was up against the wall. Like all that mattered was that I was hurting.

"He's still just Trent," Brandon goes on, and he sounds like he's trying to explain something. "Just Trent, you know?"

The car idles by the curb. I'm just standing there. The concrete is solid under my feet.

"Hey," I hear myself say, and Brandon ducks his head a little, to peer up at me again through the window. "Did I ever tell you I found out Miss Rippen's name? Or Trent did," I add, just so he knows. "Trent took a check from her at the bookstore, last week."

Silence. "No kidding," Brandon says, kind of tentative. Like, I don't know where this is heading, but I guess I'll play along. "What is it?"

"Amber."

Brandon half smiles, and then he lets himself break into a full grin. "That's a good one," he tells me. "We didn't think of that."

I take a deep breath. "You change your mind about giving out rides today?" I ask, and the words hang there like white breath in the air.

"Yeah," he says, no hesitation. "You want one?"

I don't say anything. I just reach for the handle and open the door. I slide into the leather seat, just like always. I pull the door shut, and as we're heading off down the street, I realize I'm actually kind of tired.

Like I just ran a marathon or something. And I've always thought the guys who ran marathons were nuts.

Brandon shifts, and the Corvette slips easily into the next gear. Neither of us says a word.

That's the thing about Brandon and me. It doesn't take a whole lot of words to get things said.

ABOUT THE AUTHOR

A. M. JENKINS lives in Benbrook, Texas.